The *Sky* Is Bleeding

To: Billy & Zev

Ken England

The Sky Is Bleeding

by Ken England

The Range of Insight

The Sky Is Bleeding
Copyright © 2013, Ken England
Engk Publishing

ISBN 978-0-9887741-0-0

Also by Ken England
93 Degrees

ACKNOWLEDGMENTS

I can't thank enough the team that I had working on this novel. First I would like to thank my friend, neighbor and editor Marcia Youngman, who took a lump of coal and turned it into a diamond. I also want to give my thanks to Hallie Kronebusch, a graphic artist extraordinaire. I would be remiss if I didn't give my heartfelt thanks to Shelley Sapyta from Bookmasters for her guidance through the world of publishing. Then I had an entire team of experts to guide me through the specialties of this story. Chief Master Sergeant M. Wayne Smith (Ret.) and Lieutenant Colonel Steven Smith (Ret.) helped me wade through the specifications of everything military. My friend and coworker Emergency Physician Dr. Michael Ross helped me tackle the medical issues. Penny Friend had the unenviable task of wading through this manuscript in its roughest state. Thao Do helped me understand her country of Vietnam. And of course I'm grateful to my parents, Ruth and Bob England, who are my tireless cheerleaders in everything that I undertake.

The large gray monitor lizard walked across the clearing with a robotic high step, slowly scanning the dense jungle and sampling the steamy air with its forked tongue. The immobile CIA operative sat transfixed, eyes on the lizard. With a bead of sweat rolling down his spine, he was hiding behind a mangrove shrub. The mangrove had heavy succulent leaves that barely moved in the breeze that was currently blowing. He was practiced at the stalking skills, which included the ability to sit still for an extended period of time, while he observed a one hundred and eighty degree scene. Sometimes just sitting frozen could get you more information than moving. The information would then come to you.

The lizard sensed that an intruder was nearby, but despite its stealthy movements it couldn't locate or identify the threat. Bjorn had taken the possibility of being seen into his calculations and covered his body with mud from the jungle, thus concealing odors or any visual references. He also used palm leaves to camouflage his appearance. The mud and leaves on his skin made insects less likely to find the source of their curiosity. He watched as the lizard reached about a third of the way across the clearing.

Bjorn was staring at the lizard. Suddenly he heard the droning of the C-130's engines, as did the monitor. The operative slowly turned his head to the left to see the approaching aircraft, and his experienced ears could tell this aircraft had a heavy load, which he assumed was napalm. About the time he came to this conclusion he sprang to life, running across the clearing. The monitor also starting running as the plane began pumping its lethal rain of fire over the location.

The operative was looking up to see the burning cloud as he ran and didn't see the monitor's path was intercepting his own route. He tripped over the big lizard and fell face down as the napalm reached him. The intense burning sent searing pain through every nerve in his body.

"Stop, drop and roll." The saying was fused into his memory from early childhood.

"Stop, drop and roll" —he was already on the ground, so step one and step two were accomplished. He felt the pain on his back and was worried that he had bad burns on his back. He began a log roll across the clearing. On his third turn while his back was on the ground, a large mass of napalm which had landed on a tree branch above him finally dropped free. And Bjorn was so distracted by the pain in his back he didn't see the huge glob of flaming napalm dropping right for him. Bjorn caught it with his face; the pain in his back was replaced by an intense pain on his face. He could even smell and taste the acrid chemicals much like other fuels. He frantically tried to brush the napalm off, but to no avail. It was like someone was using a belt sander on his face.

The mud he had smeared on his body to protect himself from insects helped. Instead of a third degree burn he had a second degree. He had only one thought in mind—he had to put the fire out and squelch the pain, the ever intensifying pain. He ran and he didn't know where he was running, but within ten feet the ground dropped out from under him. He fell four feet down into the nearby river. The instantaneous relief from both the water and the cooler temperatures made him feel like he had finally caught a break from a scenario that was going downhill fast.

Once he knew he was going to survive this event, his mind started whirling like a blender. How could they have sent him to a place that was scheduled for a napalm drop? That's when he remembered, napalm drops are usually scheduled a week in advance. There was only one person that could have pulled this off! His anger raged as much as the pain in his body, and he swore he would get vengeance.

CHAPTER 1

"Why! Why do you have to go?" Karen half screamed, half cried.

"Because I am a hunter and a warrior," Bjorn replied. "And I don't have to go, I want to go, to save my country," he said, gazing at the ground and shuffling some gravel around with his toe.

"But all kinds of guys tougher than you have come home in a bag."

"Those guys were wimps, I went to school with a lot of them."

"And are you made of steel?"

"No, but I've spent nearly half of my life in the woods."

She shook her head. *I'm never going to change his mind,* she thought.

"It's not the woods, it's the jungle," she said in a lower tone.

"But I can learn the jungle."

"And what about me, am I nothing?"

"Of course not, you're my girl."

Her shoulders began to heave as the sobs shook her body. He walked forward and his arms surrounded her in a bear hug. Even though he gritted his teeth, a few tears escaped his eyes. Karen slid her fingers into Bjorn's sandy blonde hair. She closed her fingers into a fist with a handful of hair in her grasp.

Her tearful eyes looked into his blue-green eyes. His unique eyes were the first thing that attracted her to him.

"You are going to hate it when they shave your head."

"It'll grow back."

Then her lips found his, and driven by a combination of frustration and passion, their tongues explored every millimeter of the other's mouth. They had kissed before, but this time was the most intense. When they took a break, Bjorn couldn't help but notice the tingling feeling in his lips. He had kissed other girls but never had this sensation before. The desire built up to a crescendo and left the lovers breathless. His rough hands began to find their way around her body but they were very gentle and the tingling in her lips was replaced by a tingling that traveled from her breasts down.

Then Karen asked the question, "When will you be leaving?"

"Tomorrow."

Their desire exploded into an immediate need.

"Make love to me," she whispered in his ear.

"But you, you might get preg-pregnant." Bjorn stuttered, wishing he wasn't being so responsible.

"I started taking the pill."

Both of the young people scrambled to get their pants off. Then the feeling of deep pleasure encased both of them. The involuntary moans echoed around the inside of the car. Karen was surprised at Bjorn's slow practiced delivery of pleasure, and she wondered if he had experience at this. But she hadn't heard of anything, especially since he spent most of his time hunting or in the woods. His fingers found all of the pleasure spots that she knew of and a few that she didn't. The lovemaking that followed was sometimes gentle, sometimes aggressive, and both of the lovers were left breathless and wanting more.

"That was great, are you sure you want to quit?" Karen asked after the lovemaking.

"No, I don't want to quit this, but I made a commitment, so I have to go."

They lay there embraced in a hug and fell asleep in that hug.

Karen opened her eyes a slit and saw the clock on the dash of the car, 3:03 a.m. But there was something unnatural outside the vehicle. The woods around the car had an eerie green tinge to them. She slid over to the window and looked up at the sky.

"Oh, my God," she said.

Bjorn suddenly startled awake.

"What's wrong?" he asked.

"The sky," is all she muttered.

They both scrambled out of the car and stood gazing up at an incredible display of the northern lights, the undulating green waves and writhing strings hanging down illuminating the landscape. They both turned around in a full circle, surveying the entire sky.

"The sky is bleeding," Bjorn said.

"No, this . . . this is a sign that we are supposed to be together. This is our future laid out in front of our eyes."

"And we will be, baby. I promise you."

Karen reached out, hugging him tightly. She didn't know it at the time, but she would spend the rest of her life studying the aurora borealis.

CHAPTER 2

Karen couldn't go to the bus station to see Bjorn off. It was too painful for her, and her phone was ringing constantly as Bjorn tried to talk to her. Karen's mother kept encouraging her to talk to him, but she was too hurt. She felt like she had been left behind, like just another dumped girlfriend. In the end she went to the bus station to see him one last time. But she was running a little late and as she got out of her car the bus was pulling away. Bjorn, gazing out the window with a forlorn look, suddenly saw Karen crying into her hands. He jumped up from his seat and ran up to the front of the bus.

"Stop, stop, stop."

"What's wrong with you, boy?" the driver asked, hitting the brakes.

"I have to say bye to my girl, please, mister."

The door opened as the air brakes hissed.

"Hurry up, boy, you can't keep this bus waitin'."

Karen was now lost in tears and was leaning over her car. Bjorn ran over to her and grabbed her around the waist. "Don't worry, baby, I will be back."

Karen let out a slight, startled scream, then collapsed into his arms, sobbing hard now.

"Bjorn, I can't take this. You'll be so far away, in a dangerous place!"

"When I get over there they'll know what danger is."

"But I'm really scared something will happen to you."

The bus driver was honking the horn to encourage him to break off his embrace.

"I gotta go baby, that guy is going to leave without me!"

The bus started to accelerate and Bjorn tore himself away from the love of his life.

"I'll be back," he yelled, as he sprinted after the bus.

Karen was in a depressed mood for weeks after Bjorn's departure.

Nine months after Bjorn was deployed he was in a boot camp for special forces soldiers at Fort Bragg, North Carolina. He had made it into an experimental new counterterrorism group. The group of the most elite soldiers was given a very technical name of 1st Special Forces Operational Detachment–Delta. But eventually the members of this specialized group referred to themselves as The Unit.

But despite some great efforts the team never came together and Bjorn kept violating all kinds of rules. This particular night Bjorn was in the brig for the third time. This incident was due to not paying attention during a training on how to make a no match fire, which he had done many times. When the officer tried to shout him down, he responded by asking if the officer wanted him to start the fire, which led to more bravado. Then Bjorn said, "What are you going to do about it?"

The cell had a small window at the top of the wall facing east. A full moon was rising, and it cast a bright rectangle of light on the opposing wall once the electric lights had been turned off.

I wonder what Karen is doing tonight. Probably having a great time out with her friends, he thought.

Karen had been dealing with bouts of insomnia ever since Bjorn had left. Tonight was no different so she went for a walk outside. As she walked she suddenly noticed there was a full moon; it was so bright that she cast a shadow to her left side.

Wow, I really look like a bowling pin now, she thought.

But she was lucky because her pregnancy was going well.

She continued walking and said hello to some other folks, walking the other way.

This is a beautiful night, but it doesn't hold a candle to that last night that Bjorn and I had together with those powerfully beautiful northern lights, she thought. *I wonder if they will symbolize the real destiny that awaits us.*

Bjorn had written her regularly in his first boot camp for the regular army, but as he climbed the ranks the letters became less frequent, each one starting with an apology for his tardiness.

The rest of the night was a wild ride for both of them. Bjorn was dragged out of his cell with several other guys in the brig, and they had a forced march that lasted all night. Karen had a night that she would not soon forget, as well as the people she had just passed. The labor pains hit her like a wave. They called an ambulance for her and she gave birth to a beautiful little girl on the night of the full moon.

CHAPTER **3**

Bjorn Tillson had grown up on the Upper Peninsula of Michigan, which was a young boy's dream, especially if he worshiped the wilderness. He was a protégé of mountain men that he had read about and was off stalking, trapping, and hunting most of the time. He learned survival skills at an early age; by ten he was doing survival jaunts in any season. This caused a lot of anguish for his parents and resulted in near dismissal from high school. But Bjorn marched to the beat of a different drummer, and he had premonitions that this was the path he must follow. By 1959, Bjorn had turned fourteen; the Vietnam War had begun and Bjorn suddenly realized his destiny.

His father had perished on Lake Superior while working for a shipping company that hauled taconite from the Iron Range region of Minnesota down to Detroit, twenty years before the *Edmond Fitzgerald*. The ship had taken a hit by a rogue wave that sent it to the bottom. Luckily for Bjorn's mother, she got a good settlement from the shipping business's insurance company, and in addition to that she got social security income. That gave her the ability to survive. She was able to take care of Bjorn and his four siblings. Bjorn spent most of his time exploring the north woods.

His enlistment on the day of his eighteenth birthday resulted in shouting and sobs from his mother, but he kept his eye on the goal. Bjorn was proficient with a number of weapons, and while he was adept with firearms he also was practiced at making longbows, cross-bows, spear throwers, and flint points. In fact he was as close to a prehistoric man as one could be and was often ribbed in high school, which led to many fights. The fights led to threats of expulsion. By the time he had enlisted in the army, Bjorn was deft at most of the skills they would teach him in boot camp. This caught the eye of the higher ups in the military, and he was quickly promoted to a Special Forces group that was in an experimental phase.

The teenager did not play well with others, and at the risk of los-ing this young warrior to time in the brig, they promoted him again to the CIA, thus allowing him to do solitary missions. The various boot camps that he had to attend took him almost two years, during which he taught his instructors and commanders more then they taught him.

In the fall of 1965 he was deployed to Vietnam and released to the command of Harlan Mckenzie, chief of the CIA in Vietnam for the last year. Bjorn and Harlan took up a challenging stance from the start, each one trying to outdo the other. And Harlan immediately felt a threat to his command. They had constant disagreements and during the Tet New Year the chief came looking for Bjorn.

"Swede, I need you to go deep into VC territory; we have a group that keeps attacking our supply lines," Harlan said.

"I told you I am not Swedish." Bjorn replied.

"Well, I can't pronounce your name, Ben, Born, and what's the difference between Swedish, Norwegian, Scandinavian? They are all the same to me."

"Well, your last name is Mckenzie, so where do you get off," Bjorn said

"I am one hundred percent American, born and raised," Harlan retorted

"So am I."

"Ok, don't cry, Lieutenant Tillson," Harlan said, with a grin on his face. "I need you to get into Khe Sanh, because we think that base is very vulnerable. I want you to observe all enemy movements on your way there, because you know how to travel unseen through this hole."

Bjorn kept his gaze on the wall beyond Harlan.

"And, Bjorn, do you have plenty of the 'juice'?"

"Yeah, and I have a bunch of weed and a bag of syrettes just for fun."

"You know, if you losers would take this war seriously, maybe we would get somewhere."

"Maybe if you would let your operatives do their jobs without screwin' with their brains, we would get somewhere."

"We're trying to make you better soldiers. Stop fighting us and let the 'juice' do its job."

"That shit is killin' me."

"That shit made you what you are."

"No, I was so much better before I started the 'juice.'"

"Those orders came down from the top; they were trying to make super soldiers."

"Well, they missed the mark."

"You are solid muscle, you can go for three days without eating or sleeping, you're a robot."

"That's what you want, a bunch of robots."

In the 1940s the Nazis used an experimental drug, which was an amphetamine-like substance, to create super soldiers. However, they ended up with a bunch of zombie drug addicts. In the ensuing years even the United States got in on the tests and a U.S. scientist refined the formula, which was used in the Vietnam conflict. One of the biggest supporters of use of this drug, referred to as "juice," was Harlan Mckenzie, and CIA operatives were chosen for the tests because their deaths could be hidden under the cloak of secrecy.

The climate of Southeast Asia and the culture of drug use both in that region and around the world made the area the perfect environment to develop these drugs and experiment on the sacrificial lambs of the military. The only problem for Chief Mckenzie was Bjorn Tillson and several other operatives. They were eliminated one at a time mostly with bad mixes of the drug. Chief Mckenzie saw himself as the pioneering force for the development of the super soldier. The biggest problem for the chief of the CIA in Vietnam was Bjorn Tillson, who saw this as a violation of the operatives' human rights, but the definition by the CIA of these operatives was that they were expendable.

The research in which they developed the amphetamines for the super soldier was conducted in the same lab where the military scientists had developed a way to spray Agent Orange over a large area. A scientist was brought over from the United States to head the research and Chief Mckenzie was closely aligned with him. The first plan was to use the Vietcong prisoners as test subjects but that was scrubbed because the military thought they were creating monsters which could be used against the U.S. forces. But Mckenzie would not be deterred and continued the tests in secret.

"Tillson, I need you to get out in country. We have a major insurgency about to happen and you are the best. We need eyes and ears on the ground," Mckenzie said.

"Anything I need to know about this?" Bjorn asked.

"Just what I told you. There seems to be a major offensive, so I want you to go to the Khe Sanh area, find out whatever you can and report back to me as soon as you can."

"Yes, sir," Bjorn responded with a look of anger on his face.

Then, as he walked away, Mckenzie said, "Make sure you have enough of the 'juice.'"

Bjorn left the next morning, traveling unseen through the countryside of South Vietnam. He first hitched a ride deep into enemy territory with the Navy and they took him up the coast and dropped him off at a remote beach. He then met the Brown Water Navy, comprised of small boats that navigated inland waterways, and they transported him inland by Swift Boat on a river almost to the Demilitarized Zone, the line between North Vietnam and South Vietnam. Bjorn immediately faded into the jungle, and the Swift Boat spun around and made a beeline back to the base. Bjorn found his way to Khe Sanh in a day and a half and was shocked by the number of Vietcong he saw. He stayed out of their way to avoid detection. All of a sudden things got very ugly, as groups of VC continued heading to Khe Sanh, but Bjorn was limited to what he could do and headed east to avoid detection. He eventually made it back to a river and called in to the forces down south to report the huge buildup of troops in the area. Harlan Mckenzie was notified of the call and his location.

"Echo, charlie, do you copy?"

"As Chief Mckenzie walked into the radio room, he heard Bjorn's voice and nodded to the radio operator.

"Go ahead bravo, x-ray."

"Echo, charlie, have info on VC movements, do you copy?"

"Copy times five." This was typical radio lingo for a very clear signal.

"10-4 echo, charlie, massive VC buildups at the following coordinates," Bjorn said and then continued to give five coordinates in the areas he had just traveled through.

"Repeat, massive insurgency, our troops in Khe Sanh in grave danger, lots of Dac Cong and special forces in the area."

Harlan Mckenzie walked over to the radio operator and scribbled a note on a piece of paper and handed it to the operator.

The operator read the note, and looked at Harlan with his hands held palms up, as if to say, "What?"

With the mike off, Harlan said, "Remember your rank, soldier."

"Yes, Chief," the operator said, knowing full well that transmitting the information on the paper might get Bjorn killed.

"Bravo, x-ray, what's your twenty?" the operator read from the slip of paper.

Bjorn was cautiously glancing around, nervous that he might get found out by speaking on the radio. And he was wondering what was taking the operator so long. But when the operator came out with that question, he was a little shocked because he never thought he would be asked to give up his location.

"Repeat echo, charlie, unable to copy."

"What are the coordinates of your location?"

Harlan handed the radio operator another slip of paper.

"Bravo, x-ray, need your coordinates, going to do a dust off, need your info back at HQ."

Bjorn didn't like this but he figured he could get out of there before the evacuation choppers came in, and then he gave the coordinates.

That's when Bjorn heard the C-130s droning toward his location, and his life would be forever changed.

CHAPTER 4

The napalm sortie which burned Bjorn was on Monday. Bjorn's radio, which he had used to call in the coordinates of the Vietnamese commandos, had fallen out of his pocket when he tripped over the monitor lizard. Another large glob of napalm had landed on the radio and fried it. He couldn't waste any time going back for the melted chunk of plastic and wires. And because of the facial burns, which caused swelling around his eyes, he could hardly see anything; he was running blind. The cool river water reduced the swelling all over his body and allowed him to see somewhat. He had accomplished his goal of putting the fire out, and unknown to him that saved his life. On Friday the U. S. generals convened a meeting because things were going to hell.

It was the Tet Lunar New Year, and the American generals were expecting a quiet week of celebrations. What they got instead were attacks all over South Vietnam, the start of what became known as the Tet Offensive. They didn't know it at the time, but the massive offensive would last until June 9 and require a huge defensive effort.

The meeting had been going for over an hour when General Richard West asked, "Chief Mckenzie, do you have any operatives in the field?"

"Yes, sir," Harlan said, "But our best man was near the Khe Sanh area on Monday and we haven't been able to contact him since that time."

"Do you think he survived the attacks?"

"Unknown sir, but we just got word that a body was found with his dog tags on it. So we are saying MIA for now. But I'm sad to say, it's probably going to be KIA," Harlan said, with a frown on his face.

"Were you able to get any information from the agent before you lost contact?"

"Yes, sir, he called in on Monday and told us that a major offensive was under way and then no more contact."

"Where was he when he called in?"

"He was near Operation Scotland."

"And where was the body found with the dog tags?"

"The body was found on a river just south of Operation Scotland; looks like he was trying to escape."

"Who found the body?" the general asked.

"A Swift Boat crew."

"What was the apparent cause of death?' another general asked.

"It's hard to say, but because the body was badly burned we are calling it napalm."

"What was he doing in a place that was going to get a napalm drop!?" The general asked, somewhat exasperated.

"General, Lieutenant Tillson was somewhat of a loose cannon. He often did things by his own rules."

"Damn CIA, can't live with them, can't live without them."

"Also, there was another soldier found with Lieutenant Tillson."

"Dead?"

"No, sir, this soldier is alive and in the MASH unit, also with burns."

"Could we verify the ID of the dead soldier?"

"Hard to say, General, the body was badly decomposed, but the dog tags were those of my missing operative." the chief said. "I'm going to go to that MASH unit as soon as I can to check IDs."

"Negative, Chief, with this new VC offensive, we are going to need all available operatives, so don't waste your time with worthless things, get your men in the field," the general said.

"Yes, sir," Chief Mckenzie said.

As Harlan left the meeting he thought, *That's bullshit. Tillson left for his mission just four days before that body was found, there's no way his corpse could have rotted that much. He switched dog tags with that dead soldier.*

CHAPTER 5

After the napalm attack Bjorn had drifted down river, eventually finding a floating log, which he threw his arms over and subsequently lost consciousness. Eventually the log bumped onto a sandbar, where it stayed. Bjorn came around and crawled up onto the sandbar to die. The cool water had brought down the swelling on his face, so he could see again. During his brief bout of consciousness he had the wherewithal to look around at his surroundings.

As if the start of this episode wasn't shocking enough, he saw a body and crawled over to the rotting corpse. It was apparent that the body had been there for sometime and had been the feast of animals and insects of the area. The fatigues told Bjorn that it had been a United States combatant and then he saw the dog tags. He slipped his own tags off and gingerly swapped his with the dead soldier's. He quickly looked at the tags that he had just acquired. Bjorn had a complete identity change. He was now Larry Johns. Score two points, first the cool bath and now this identity transformation. He dragged himself away from the stench and accepted the fact that he might never wake up from this nightmare, then lost consciousness again.

The lookout on the Swift Boat shouted, "Captain, DB on the right shore, no, I think there are two DBs."

"Fifties, keep your eyes peeled, this could be a trap!" the captain shouted.

The two gunners on the sides of the boat cocked their weapons and spotters walked over next to them to help keep watch on the shoreline.

As the boat lost speed the bow dropped down and the captain reversed the engines to keep from grounding.

"Medic, check those soldiers."

The medic jumped into the knee-deep water and waded ashore. As he approached the bodies he was repulsed by the look of the man's back. Raw patches of tissue and large blisters were visible and a number of flies took to flight from the man's back as the medic approached. The sight made the medic feel a little nauseated, but what almost put him over the top were several leeches that were feeding on the raw wounds.

He then walked over to the other body and noted that there was a lot of decomposition and it had almost skeleton-like features; this one was definitely dead. The medic walked back to the first body and was amazed by what looked like the rise and fall of his back. He laid his shoulder bag of medical supplies down on the sand. Then he slid a hand under the comatose man's broad shoulder to roll him over. As the man lying on the sand was flipped over two things startled the medic. First the man's face was badly scarred and blistered and some sand was stuck to what skin he had left. But the scariest thing was the guttural scream that emitted from the man. The medic tripped over the medical bag as he jumped back.

The other sailors on the Swift Boat were riveted by the developments.

"You two," the captain shouted, looking at the spotters, "get down there and help him get that man on board."

As the three sailors struggled to carry the wounded soldier to the boat, some skin on Bjorn's arm peeled off in the rescuer's hand, which made the man vomit into the river. Finally Bjorn was on board. The medic started intravenous lines of fluid and gave the wounded man a good dose of morphine. Then the boat headed back to the base at high speed.

Bjorn woke up three days later as the sedatives and morphine wore off and the nurses were cleaning his burns. Possibly the worst part of the experience for him was not the pain but the smell of his own burned flesh and especially the thought of being burned on his face. The smell was ever present and one thing that was in short supply in Vietnam was air freshener. The smell sometimes would migrate from his nose down into his mouth and the taste often made him feel nauseated. The smell was almost like his skin was rotting even through the nurses did a good job of debriding the burns and keeping them clean. He moaned somewhat and one of the nurses started to run for the doctor, but he grabbed her arm. She stopped and looked back at the disfigured man in the bed. Several people from the upper ranks of the military had visited the man. It looked like they were searching for information and not making a sympathy gesture. They made sure the nurses contacted them if the soldier woke up.

The nurse turned and said, "Hello, Sergeant, can I call you Larry?"

He just looked at the nurse and their eyes connected. She was stunned by the beauty of his eyes but also repulsed because the eyes were surrounded by a face that was almost devoid of normal skin. Then he glanced down at the dog tags lying on his chest. And realized his ruse was still working.

"I'm a horrible mess, aren't I?"

"Oh, don't say that, sweetie, when you get home your family will surround you with love. It will take some time, but you will recover and people will accept you."

"They won't even recognize me."

"Honey, it's not how you look, but what you do that really matters, so dedicate your life to helping others and you will be reborn."

"I need some painkillers."

"Okay, I'll call the doctor, but I need to find out your pain level."

"The pain is bad."

"How about on a one to ten scale."

"Ten."

"Well, okay, Larry," she said in her southern drawl. "I'll get the doctor."

Bjorn thought about Karen. *I was such an idiot thinking that I could fix the world and that I was immortal. I should have stayed in Michigan with Karen, by now we would be starting a family. Instead, here I am, a monster that no one will even get close to. I could have had heaven and I chose hell. I can't try to see Karen, if she thinks I'm dead she will go on with her life. Yes, that will be the best.*

Bjorn closed his eyes when he heard footsteps approaching. "Sergeant Johns, can you open your eyes?" The doctor's voice came out loud and clear. But Bjorn, feigning unconsciousness, kept his eyes closed and did not respond.

Finally the doctor said, "Okay, Nurse, give him some more morphine."

The nurse continued to wrap his burns with the roller bandages as had been done so many times before. He drifted off into a drug-induced slumber. Then the delusions started again, whenever he got morphine and was alone in his room the visions would start. This time Harlan Mckenzie appeared in his dreams, and he was smoking a big Cuban cigar and laughing, then Harlan said, "Don't worry, he won't survive those burns."

Bjorn forced himself awake and realized he had soaked his bandages with his sweat. He feared he was becoming addicted to the morphine. At that point he began hatching a plan. A fellow patient that had been transferred out because he had developed a severe infection and that gave Bjorn an idea. The next time they put him on the bedpan and left the room, Bjorn reached down into the pan with his index finger then slid his finger between the bandages on his back. He did this several times over the next few days. By the next week, the doctor that took a look at his burns gave the nurse a new order.

"I want this patient to receive two liters of Ampicillin IV, and let's start to taper down on the morphine."

"Yes, doctor."

When he was alone Bjorn unplugged the IV line and the antibiotic drained down into a trash can. Then when the bag was almost empty he reattached it. Within another week the doctor said, "We are not controlling this infection, so I want this patient to be on the next flight to Ramstein

Air Force Base. I will do the paperwork, and that way we will have another bed open up."

As Bjorn arrived in Ramstein, he could feel a huge weight lift off his shoulders. Even though he was not afraid of Harlan, he knew the chief could do whatever he wanted. Being thousands of miles away from Vietnam allowed him to sleep without worrying about waking up with a knife in his chest.

The surgeon at Ramstein Air Force Base was a major in the United States Army. When he unwrapped Bjorn's bandages he didn't like the look of the abscesses on the soldier's cheeks. "Sergeant Johns, these blister-like sores on your face are not a good sign."

"So what do you want to do, cut my face off?"

"Well, in a sense, yes," the surgeon said.

Bjorn was laughing. "Come on, seriously."

"I would like to excise those two abscesses on your cheeks and because of the size of them, I am planning on putting skin grafts over the two areas that I remove," he explained.

"I look that bad, huh."

"Sergeant, it's not a matter of looks, but I'm concerned about the infections, the antibiotics are not keeping up with the infections and if we don't act now, you may develop sepsis, and shortly after that you will be a statistic."

"How good are you?" Bjorn asked.

"How good am I?"

"That's my question."

"I've been a military surgeon for ten years. I've done many skin grafts because this war is producing a lot of burns."

"Why are you still in the military? You would do much better in the private sector."

"My wife is one of the nurses here and I'm just here, killing time."

"Oh, bad choice of words," Bjorn said, laughing, but laughter caused pain so he cut the laugh short. He had to concentrate to remember the change of his name and when everybody called him Larry, it took him a second to respond.

"So, what do you think, Larry?"

"Alright, let's get on with it, and I will need some more pain medication."

"We will take care of your pain before, during and after your surgery."

"Sounds good."

"So listen, Larry, did you know Lieutenant Tillson?"

Bjorn froze and he could feel his heart pounding. "No, I'm not sure who you are talking about."

"His body was right next to yours on that sandbar."

Bjorn nervously looked around, expecting a trap. He knew the CIA had a very long arm.

"No, that guy was there for days before I washed up on the sandbar."

"Well, I heard he was a legend in Vietnam, he had many exploits that are making the rounds. Too bad he had to die."

"Really, I didn't know him." Bjorn said. He was a little pissed that he couldn't take credit for his hard work during the war.

"Okay, we will have you in surgery in a couple hours."

"Great, and don't forget my pain medication."

A nurse came into his room and injected a syringe with 2 milligrams of morphine into the IV line. Bjorn was asleep when they rolled him into the operating room. The anesthetist put him under and the surgery started. The surgeon began excising the infected parts of his face and found more damage then anticipated. So the removal was further out then first thought. While the surgeon was working on Bjorn's face, another surgeon was removing flaps of skin from both thighs. Then at about two hours into the surgery they sutured the flaps onto his face.

The healing took six months and then Bjorn was flown back to the air force base in Dover, Delaware, where all returning soldiers are outprocessed and released back into society. However, he returned as Larry Johns. Bjorn's family was told that he was killed in action.

CHAPTER 6

KIA: those three letters were burned forever into Karen's subconsciousness. It was the worst acronym she could have heard. What was she supposed to do now except go over to see Bjorn's mother and brothers and offer her condolences. No one could give her any answers mostly because she wasn't family, but even his family was in the dark. When Karen tried to talk to Bjorn's mother all she would say is, "He's in God's hands."

The first information from the military was missing in action, MIA, and Karen knew Bjorn and knew his skills; she had a feeling that he was still alive. But when the letters changed to KIA, all her hope dissolved. A military detail consisting of a Casualty Assistance Officer, the Squadron Commander and a Chaplain were sent to Bjorn's house, and his mother collapsed and his next younger brother broke three fingers when he punched the lath and plaster wall in the house. That hole in the wall stayed there for many years after that.

"Hi, Baby, I told you I was coming back for you," Bjorn said. Karen jolted awake with tears in her eyes—the dreams were torture. And they continued for almost a year.

"Karen, it has been a month, you have got to lift yourself up by your bootstraps and get on with your life!"

"Mom! My boyfriend was killed in Vietnam!"

"That's right and your father was killed while he was working on Lake Superior, but I had two kids to take care of and I couldn't sit around crying."

"Thanks for the support, Mom. And thanks for reminding me that I have a black cloud hanging over me."

"What are you talking about?"

"Everyone I get close to comes to some kind of disastrous end."

"Everyone you are close to, that says a lot about me, doesn't it?"

"You know what I mean!"

"I will not enable your depression, so I'm giving you a dose of reality."

"All I'm trying to do is wrap my brain around this."

"You have lost your father and your boyfriend, you have to understand that life and death are one and the same!"

"They are not the same thing."

"One always follows the other. They are unfortunately linked."

"So what am I supposed to do, throw a party?"

"Yes, and celebrate the good times you had with Bjorn, and celebrate his life."

"But, Mom, that war was useless, there was no reason to throw those boys lives away."

"And I agree with that, but we have a lot of freedoms in this country because our soldiers fight for our freedom."

"But that still doesn't bring Bjorn back."

"I know, but you are young and beautiful and you will find another boyfriend. Also now you have responsibilities that you didn't have before. That child needs you to be there for her."

Karen just shook her head and stormed out of the house, and while she was walking she realized her mother was right. She couldn't just sit around pouting. Within a month she was enrolled in the University of Colorado, studying astronomy. She wanted to study the northern lights, but she had to start with astronomy for her undergrad degree. But things were very difficult; classes were harder then she anticipated. And since boyfriends were less capable than she expected, she decided she would have to go solo for awhile or stop comparing everyone to Bjorn. She dedicated her life to two things, her schoolwork and raising her daughter.

Eventually she did meet a young man who was in the astronomy program with her. He was a very intelligent man who maintained a 4.0 grade point average. However, Clyde was a geek: he studied astronomy, talked astronomy and lived astronomy. When Karen wanted a kiss or a hug or anything else she nearly had to write a thesis. But Karen saw him as the secure provider that she needed. The sex wasn't the greatest, but Clyde didn't have time to study the *Kama Sutra*. Clyde was an inexperienced and quick lover; he was in it for the ride, without any consideration of what gave Karen pleasure. And Karen had a lot going on in her life, with a young daughter, school and work, all of which she had to handle herself.

Two years later they both graduated from their undergraduate work and were married. On the day of her marriage Karen knew she had made a mistake. However, she decided to work hard on the relationship to make it work. She decided that sex was no longer an issue for her and ultimately took care of herself, most of the time. Clyde and Karen started trying to add to their family at that point. But after two more years, Karen's OB/GYN doctor told her she would never have any more children.

That news made Clyde start thinking about some other choices, but he wanted a child with his own DNA. Therefore the marriage was doomed to failure.

CHAPTER 7

When the ex–CIA operative, ex–special forces soldier left Dover, Delaware, with his discharge papers, he also left with a grudge, and a new name. He felt a lot of animosity towards the military, the United States and, of course, toward a certain CIA chief. The anger was eating him up and he knew he had to let go of it or it would kill him. There was one more thing that Bjorn left with, and that was an addiction to opiates, which controlled his life.

Towards the end of his burn treatment, he could handle the pain but would act like the pain was unbearable to keep receiving the morphine. But even before the burn he had been set up for addiction by the use of the amphetamines, and part of him still longed for the rush of the drugs.

Once he got out into society after the drug-fueled sixties, he realized that drugs were easy to come by. He started with marijuana and then worked up through increasingly hard drugs, and he would try anything. And while alcohol didn't have the effect he wanted, in the absence of hard drugs, Bjorn would choose alcohol and even got drunk on a bottle of Listerine but had to drink a whole bottle to get a moderate high.

When he could get harder drugs like cocaine, he was much better off, but still wasn't satisfied without the really hard drugs such as the morphine that had gotten him into this downward spiral. When he could get it, he would shoot heroin because he always wanted more.

He had drifted around the country stealing money to feed his addiction, spending time in jails, until the cops in one town bought him a bus ticket to another town, so they wouldn't have to deal with him. One day he woke up in a Detroit crack house. He was nauseated and tried to make it to the bathroom to vomit, but the water to the house had been shut off. And the toilet was full of human feces. That made him vomit even more as he hovered above the excrement.

He got into an argument with another guy in the house.

"You have to give me some money so I can get a fix," the other man said.

"I don't have to give you shit," Bjorn said.

"I paid the last time, it's your turn."

"You know I don't have any money."

The man lunged at Bjorn with a knife and Bjorn's training kicked in and he was able to disarm him and put the man down on the ground. Then he shook his head to try and clear it and when he opened his eyes, he realized he was still sitting beside the stool-filled toilet. There was no other man, no knife and he was alone in the house. He often had these visions, and when they were over he knew he had to quell his mind spinning out of control. He hitchhiked north to the Upper Peninsula and was kicked out of several rides for vomiting out the window.

When he got to his hometown of Sault Ste. Marie in the Upper Peninsula, he went to the fast food restaurant where Karen had worked and asked for her. But the girl behind the counter said, "I'm sorry, sir, she's not here anymore, she left to go to college."

"Where is that?" Bjorn asked.

"Boy, I don't know, somewhere in the Southwest," she said with a smile on her face.

Man that guy was a mess, looked like he had puked on himself, she thought after he left.

He sat down outside on a bench and realized he needed help. He was penniless, without a home or friends. He was desperate and decided he had to go back to his family. He walked up to his house and rang the doorbell A young man of about seventeen years old opened the door, and the boy, even though older than the last time he saw him, looked like his younger brother. Bjorn had sunglasses on to hide the obvious sign of pinpoint pupils, indicating he was high.

"Can I help you, sir?"

"Yes, I'm Bjorn, I'm your brother!"

The boy looked at the man standing on his doorstep and thought he looked like death warmed over. The boy, who had large shoulders and was very muscular, was probably in high school sports, judging by his physical stature. The boy became very angry and said, "How dare you impersonate my brother."

"No, no," Bjorn sputtered out, "I went to Vietnam and now I'm back."

"Look, I don't know who you are, but my brother died in Vietnam, and just because you know a few things about him doesn't mean you can come here and pretend to be him."

"No, you don't understand."

"I don't understand, no, I understand all I need to understand, and if you don't want me to kick your ass, then you'd better get out of here."

Then he slammed the door in Bjorn's face, and the former special forces and CIA operative became an ex-son and ex-brother to the people he had grown up with. He was shocked beyond belief and stood there for a moment trying to figure out what to do. But Bjorn had just lost his connection to the human race, and now he had nothing to live for. So he stumbled into a convenience store and shoplifted a pack of razors and walked out to the parking lot. Then he slit both wrists and lay there bleeding. A customer came running into the store and shouted, "Call 911."

An ambulance responded and rushed him to the hospital, applying direct pressure the whole way. When the apparently homeless man arrived at the hospital, he had no identification or money, and when the doctor examined him he saw the tracks from IV drug use and had the homeless man committed to an institution for evaluation.

Bjorn spent a month there, after which time the therapist decided that there was no reason to keep him. At that point the director of the institution called the police and asked them to take Bjorn to the Canadian border. And that was fine with him because he had been wanting to become an expatriate for some time now. The police did so gladly because that was one less hassle for them to deal with.

They dropped him off about a mile from the border and Bjorn walked east until he got to the shore of Lake Superior. He was trying to figure out how to head north. But first he met some kids that were planning a party on a beach on the Canadian coastline. They had several motor boats and found a secluded beach on the Canadian shoreline and then the party got under way in earnest. It lasted all night and by the morning all the kids had left and Bjorn was alone on the beach. He had fallen into the drug trap again, first with pot and then with Quaaludes, followed by a small amount of cocaine. When he woke up he was hung over and unsure of where he was. That's when his survival training kicked in and he began making a plan.

He knew he had to shake this monkey off his back, because it was killing him. He started walking north, using his survival skills to stay alive. He still had a need to get high and had to fight that desire with all his might because this fight to stay alive was enough of a challenge that he didn't want drugs to complicate things, and there weren't a lot of natural drugs in the north woods of Ontario. Eventually he found a job on a garbage truck, but he knew being in society again would be a disaster for him and he knew he had to get out. He found a lot of clothes while working for the garbage company and often spent nights in the local landfill because the rotting garbage had some warmth to it.

He worked just long enough to acquire the money to get the tools and equipment he needed, and then he got a ride to the Missinaibi River and canoed the three hundred miles to Hudson Bay. The river was mostly gentle and when he encountered aggressive white water he portaged around it. Kettle Falls was the first white water, twenty miles in, and the addiction was still dragging him down. He was fighting the shaking frenzies, and one warm day he paddled over to a gray rock which was ramping down into the river and climbed out and collapsed there with tremors. A few hours later he was brought back to consciousness by the haunting, mournful call of a loon, and upon opening his eyes, he realized the rock he was lying on was etched in a gridlike pattern. It looked a lot like the pattern of skin grafts on his back and face. He realized this pattern was from the extreme glaciation that had occurred during the last ice age, when the glaciers gouged the Precambrian rock of the Canadian Shield. Eventually he dragged himself back to his canoe and continued paddling, all the while wondering when he would be free of these symptoms.

One of the biggest challenges was the black flies, mosquitoes and other insects. He lived in a head net. In a strange way his injury was a gift when it came to the insects because the nerves had been destroyed by the burns. Whenever he encountered big white water, he had three choices: to paddle it, line the boat around it or to portage, to carry the boat on a trail around the rapids.

He was carrying his canoe down such a trail, and because the trail was on tundra, the traffic from people walking down this trail had caused the fragile land to break down into a bog. His first few steps were a little mushy, and then he suddenly sank up to his knees in black mud. The weight on his back forced him deeper, down to midthigh. He quickly flipped the canoe off his shoulders and then set his pack in the boat. He was still stuck in a quicksand-like bog and the only way to get out of it was to lean onto the boat. But then another problem came up. As he fought to pull his feet up out of the bog, he felt his foot leaving his shoe. As he slowly pulled his feet out, it produced a suction sound. When he finally got his feet out of the bog, his left foot was shoeless. That meant he had to lie down across the boat and reach his arm down into the hole that his leg had just left, and he had to do it before the hole closed. Finally his hand touched his shoe down in the hole, but the tug of war had just begun. The mud had closed in around his arm so with his other hand he dug a bigger hole and eventually he broke the suction and extracted his mud-covered shoe. He knew from his past that the hardest part of any adventure was often the part that was least expected, and that was certainly true of his battle with the bog.

After a two-mile portage at Thunderhouse Falls he put the boat back into a quiet eddy, and as he pushed off he saw some color on the rock cliff. He paddled over to the cliff and looked at the wall. The rock paintings were vibrant compared to the gray rock and depicted several humans, one that looked like he had flames coming off of his body as he ran. At that point Bjorn knew that his Canadian journey was the right thing to do and maybe this was a signal from an ancient culture. As he looked around at the land after the large rock vein which had caused the falls, the land continued on like before, which was the thick shield of rock covered by a small amount of earth with huge blue spruces growing out of the thin soil. Spruces sent their roots out horizontally, so a huge tree could be supported by a small amount of earth. However, he often saw large trees blown over by a particularly forceful wind.

His goal was not to be a hero but just get from point A to point B, and his canoeing skills were a little rusty. The most important part of the trip was it completely changed his way of thinking. He often woke up with night sweats because of the withdrawal he was dealing with but they eventually subsided. Over the two weeks that it took him to canoe to Hudson Bay, he had gone through a complete transformation. While he knew he would never be completely free of the addiction, there was nothing to get high on in the wilderness he was passing through. Eventually, his addictive need was replaced by the desire to start a new life.

At times when he was canoeing on quiet waters and his powerful arms dipped the paddle in the water time and time again, he felt a feeling of release. Occasionally he would lie back in the boat and just drift with the current, and in his mind he knew that this was the right choice to be here. He had gotten low on food and had to rely on a lichen called rock tripe that grew on the rocks around the area. It was a little difficult to swallow but when he used his spices and filleted a fish that he had caught it became tolerable. Then when he got to Hudson Bay along the shores of Polar Bear Provincial Park, there was a strong east to west wind blowing. That created waves of at least eight feet and Bjorn decided that this would be a good time to stop and he took this as a premonition, that this should be his new home.

Then he travelled up the west shore of the bay. At the place where the Winisk River flowed into the bay, he located a site to build a cabin so he could live out his life without being bothered or die trying. He found a bench that would be perfect to build a cabin on. It looked down on the Winisk River, and to the east was the huge expanse of the inland sea known as Hudson Bay. Harrison Canyon was three hundred feet deep and his bench was only fifty feet up. It was the perfect place because it was protected from storms and floods, and there was ample timber all around. Bjorn got to work on constructing his small cabin. The only problem was this bench was also the home of a wolverine. And when Bjorn set up camp there, the brutish creature charged him with a hopping step as it made a huffing noise. The animal was small enough to be dispatched with an axe but it had the attitude of a bull and didn't fear anything. Eventually the wolverine acquiesced and wandered off to find a new home, but for days after that Bjorn never went anywhere without his axe. The roar of a distant waterfall on the Winisk provided the white noise that put him to sleep every night.

Harrison Canyon was named after William Henry Harrison, who helped settled these territories and went on to be the U.S. president with the shortest term in history. The canyon had been cut by the Winisk over millions of years of erosion. The canyon was impressive and was close to the Grand Canyon of the north country and had several huge drops, resulting in some outstanding waterfalls as it dropped off the Canadian Shield. The Winisk River had been named by the Cree Indians and its fish provided a good food supply for Bjorn. He also had access to good hunting and was out hunting one day. He was hidden in a small grove of trees when a herd of caribou came by, a bull following several does in his harem. Bjorn quickly notched an arrow in his bow and drew the longbow back as far as he could. He aimed at a forty-five degree angle as he followed the buck and then let the arrow fly. The animals froze when they heard the twang of the bow; Bjorn had anticipated that and in five seconds the arrow hit the bull and pierced both of his lungs the herd panicked and started running. The bull managed to take ten steps before plowing into the snow.

That's when Bjorn first saw the huge bear.

Bjorn first looked around to see if anything or anyone was watching him and saw nothing. Then he got his weapons together and began to approach his prey, his mukluks with seal skin soles falling silently on the tundra. He felt a warm breeze blow into his face.

Too warm for March, he thought.

The winter had been warmer than any he had ever experienced. None of the Inuit hunters in the area could explain this unusual weather. His meat stores in his raised meat storage locker had started to spoil.

This one hunt will take care of me for months, he thought exultantly.

As he walked he notched another arrow in his bow; the animal could still be alive and that rack could do some damage.

Suddenly, a white flash exploded from a thicket just to the north of the wounded bull. Bjorn jumped into a defensive stance, startled by the loud noise and the white blur which flashed across his visual field.

Once he got his wits about him, with his longbow fully drawn he aimed at the fast-moving flash. He focused on what was going on about forty yards in front of him. It was a polar bear that had been laying in wait for the approaching caribou. The bear had not yet seen Bjorn and was totally focused on the meal laying there waiting for him. This was not just any bear; even from forty yards, it was huge. And for its size it was extremely agile. Bjorn had slowly begun to crouch down to hide himself behind some low shrubs. The bear tore

the flank from the caribou, ripping off a huge chunk of meat and consumed it in a few seconds.

This guy is hungry, Bjorn thought. *Must be due to the warm weather,
polar bears usually hunt from the ice for ring seals, but the warmer weather
was preventing that.*

The polar bear continued tearing large gaping holes in the flank
of the bull, and then it noticed the arrow protruding from the animal's rib cage. Bjorn watched every move in complete silence but
started to lift the large spear off his shoulder as the bear sniffed the
shaft and feathers. The animal stood up to his full height and began
to scan the horizon. The hunter froze completely, still watching but
trying not to lock gazes with the bear. Predators react very poorly to
that and Bjorn didn't want to be on this bear's butt-kicking list. The
animal's head was easily ten feet from the ground. It towered above
the tundra and continued to scan the surrounding countryside. Its
face was completely red with blood. Then its gaze stopped on the
small hiding place that was concealing Bjorn. Neither hunter moved
for an exceedingly long time.

Then the bear went back to feasting. Bjorn was beginning to get
stiff from crouching in the cool arctic air. Finally the bear grabbed
what was left of the caribou and started walking toward the canyon,
dragging the corpse along with it. Not knowing the bear was hiding
nearby had been Bjorn's first mistake. Then he made another bad
decision. He started following the trail created by the tracks and the
bloody half-eaten caribou. Bjorn had decided to observe this incredible animal some more, thinking he might never have another chance.
But then he changed his mind as he approached Harrison Canyon.
He wasn't really prepared for this suicide mission.

CHAPTER **8**

His life of isolation was very difficult. The summers were tough and the winters worse. In the summers the mosquitoes, black flies and the no-see-um's were brutal. One trick to deal with the insects was to smear mud on any exposed skin, thus creating a shield between the pests and skin. The winters added their own challenges with the extreme cold which was slowly changing to a moderate cold, with occasional bouts of extreme cold. The twenty below days would burn any exposed skin and he was especially vulnerable because his skin was damaged. Bjorn was barely surviving, even though he was as close to an expert at survival as anyone. What he regretted the most was his decision to go fight the war; if he knew that this was going to be the result he would have never enlisted. He had no nearby neighbors, no companionship. He missed Karen intensely. How could he have walked away from that night of sweet loving?

That's when Sarah changed everything. Sarah was young but somewhat disenchanted, once she realized the cruelness of people was aimed at her. She became suicidal during her early teens and finally decided that she would escape to the north country to seek solace. She had a canoe and decided a solo canoe trip down the Winisk River in Ontario would be just what the doctor ordered. She planned every detail, down to the smallest minutiae. If something terrible happened and she lost her life that was just a different means to an end. When she got to the mouth of the river earlier than she'd planned, she decided to canoe along the shore of Hudson Bay.

Bjorn was stalking caribou, using his time-tested hunting technique of sitting quietly and observing. The only challenge was the cloud of black flies that had formed around his head with the occasional suicidal fly that dove into his eye or up his nose. He had stationed himself at the mouth of the canyon where the river entered the bay. Suddenly he was aware of a single canoeist working his way down the shore, and even more shocking than seeing another person was the scraping noise as the canoe beached very close to Bjorn. All of a sudden he realized he wasn't alone, and he might have to interact with someone. He didn't move but became a little intrigued when he saw the solo canoeist had mud smeared on his face to protect him from the insects. That was Bjorn's trick.

Sarah was sweating hard because of a headwind and decided to clean up. She went ashore near the mouth of the river. The canoeist began to disrobe and Bjorn felt a stirring in his loins for the first time in many years, when the body of the canoeist turned out to be, without a doubt, that of a woman's. And a very attractive woman. There was one interesting thing, and that was some extreme sunburn down the right side of her body. As she washed the mud off her face, he could see the burn went up to her face. He had never seen that before. The purplish skin covered 25 to 30 percent of the right side of her body.

Sarah was oblivious to the accidental voyeur, and he was clueless that he was doing anything wrong, so he decided he would remain motionless until she left because if she didn't know, then no harm no foul. That's when all his plans came crashing down. Bjorn quickly notched an arrow, and with the weapon drawn he came bursting out of the underbrush.

"What are you doing?" Sarah screamed as she quickly grabbed her clothes and pressed them against her naked body.

Bjorn stared half at her, half over her head.

"Are you some kind of a freak?" she stammered out.

"Ursa, you back off, this one is mine, you can have the caribou I just saw." Bjorn stated with authority.

"What do you mean, this one is yours? I don't belong to anybody."

"You would be better off being quiet." He said with the arrow still aimed slightly over her head.

She stared at him and then heard a slight moaning behind her. When she turned around she saw an off-white wall of fur. Her gaze continued up until her eyes fell upon the face of an adult polar bear, a full ten feet above the ground.

"Don't make eye contact with him, it will be perceived as a threat." Bjorn said.

She did him one better; the site of this monstrosity took her breath away and she dropped to her knees, expecting death at any moment. Ursa, the name Bjorn had given the creature, stared down at the tiny crumbled human at his feet, then started shaking his head back and forth as if to say that he would not be defeated, but Bjorn kept a constant conversation with him in a casual low voice. Then the bear dropped down to all fours and ambled off, complaining as he went.

Bjorn was finally able to release the tension on the longbow and jumped down to where Sarah was. When he lifted her up into his arms, she slid an arm around his neck and pulled him closer. He carried Sarah back to his cabin and made her comfortable on the bed in his cabin, and he slept on a pad on the floor. In the morning he was startled awake as he heard the door close.

"Where are you going?" he shouted as he ran out of the cabin.

"I've been too much of a burden on you," she replied.

"Don't be ridiculous. I saved your life and this is the thanks I get."

"Yeah, you and your pet bear," Sarah retorted.

"Ursa is a wild animal, we just happen to hunt the same land."

"Yeah, right, and how did you teach him English?"

"We just have a mutual understanding and I know how animals behave and react."

"What would you have done if the bear wanted a snack?"

"We would have both died then. Even if I could have placed that arrow perfectly, I'm sure you could tell that Ursa is an unprecedented specimen, the likes of which has never before been seen, and he would have killed both of us."

Sarah whirled around and that was the first time she had gotten a good look at his face. Bjorn had a full beard that was a little patchy and the skin around his beard was scarred. She stood speechless as she studied him.

"You sure that the bear didn't smack you around?"

Bjorn started laughing in a boisterous, booming laugh. "No, I was burned when I was younger; you should see my back. And you fly too close to the sun?"

Sarah smiled, "Yeah, you can call me Icarus."

"I'd rather call you by your real name," Bjorn replied.

"I'm Sarah," she said as she walked forward to shake hands. That's the first time she saw his intensely shining eyes.

"I'm Bjorn."

"You're what?"

He smiled again and she realized his eyes flamed brighter every time he smiled. "My family is from Norway and they called me Bjorn."

"Well, that's a beautiful name. And as far as this," she said, touching her face, "this is a birthmark, they call it port wine stain, and if I could get drunk off of it, we could be having a grand time right now." They both chuckled.

Sarah slept on the floor that night and neither of them got much sleep. Sarah was nervous being in the lair of someone she didn't know and kept her fishing knife close to her. Bjorn was afraid that he would screw up this opportunity, as he had done with Karen, and that fear was realized the very next morning.

Bjorn was up and moving around the cabin when Sarah woke up, packed her bags, and walked out the door. He ran outside to see her headed down to her canoe.

"Now where are you going?" he shouted

"I don't want to ruin your single life," she replied.

"I didn't say you were ruining anything."

"No, but I can tell, me being here would change everything."

Yeah, for the better, he thought.

He watched dumbfounded as she loaded her canoe, pushed it into the water, and started paddling away.

For the life of me I cannot figure women out; it must be my burns. But with her disfigurement, I thought we would be perfect for each other.

If I can keep him guessing I'll have a little more control over this situation, Sarah thought as she paddled away. Besides, I have to meet my flight out of here.

Two days later a floatplane landed on the bay to take Sarah and her gear back to civilization.

"I thank you guys for flying in here, but I found a cabin back aways and I'm going to spend more time out here."

"Are you sure about that?" one of the pilots asked.

"Yup, I've had a great time up here, and you can keep the money since I wasted your time."

Both men just stared at each other slack jawed.

"Okay, ma'am, if you say so," one pilot said.

Bjorn heard a distant plane taking flight. "That was a once in a lifetime chance, and I don't know how I blew it."

The next day Sarah paddled back to his cabin and walked up on the porch.

"Okay, I've decided to stay but there are going to be rules."

All Bjorn could do was nod his head. The two of them stared at each other and while neither of them would say it, each one knew that they had found their soulmate.

The relationship started off as just an agreement. They would work together to survive in this potentially harsh and foreboding land.

CHAPTER 9

The first months of Karen's time at the Mees Observatory were difficult, mostly because she was a woman in a man's world and also because her theories on solar storms were threatening to the standard theories. Karen was the first to state and ultimately prove that solar storms could have devastating effects on satellites and even aircraft. She always cited the Skylab disaster and suspected a lot of other tragedies were the result of the radiation and wild magnetic waves entering the atmosphere. She said that Skylab's demise was due to construction shortfalls that weren't acted on until the satellite was in orbit. Karen had studied the project as an undergraduate, so she knew about the shortcuts that NASA had undertaken. She was working on her PhD when the space station came down and as far as she was concerned that was proof of her research. Skylab had been damaged on launch, which was devastating, because there was a solar observatory on board and she needed it to complete her PhD, but did confirm coronal holes in the Sun. All of these factors culminated in Skylab's fall from orbit and was a setback to her research.

She entered a world where she had a lot to prove, both to herself and to the other astrophysicists.

Thus she had to work three times as hard as any of the men. She had moved from Kitt Peak Observatory in Taos, New Mexico, to Mees Observatory in Maui, where they had an active solar program that gave the telescope some use during the day, as well as the nighttime.

Mees Observatory was Karen's dream job and it was in a place that wasn't too hard to live in. Her marriage to Clyde was over, but he was well known throughout astronomy circles.

The year was 1977. After two years of fighting the establishment, Karen had gotten some respect, mostly because her theories were starting to prove themselves in the upper tiers of the bureaucracy. Luna was ten years old, and in fifth grade. She was also riding a wave up the ladder of surfing competition, and she was getting very good on a surfboard. The ribbons were starting to collect on her bedroom wall.

Karen dated as much as she could, but it was difficult with a ten-year-old because she had to set up a sitter, and with moving around to different areas it was hard to find dates. But once she accepted the fact that she would have to make a choice between romance and motherhood, the scientist focused on being the best mother that she could be. Many men in the footloose and fancy free crowd in Hawaii were put off by a woman with a ten-year-old child.

As Luna grew, though, she moved further away from her mother, as most children do. So Karen spent more and more time alone in their house, wondering where her daughter was. But she knew a parent has to be careful not to control a child but to oversee from a distance. And since Karen was focused on climbing the ladder of this technical, scientific world where everyone spoke in code, she had a hard time understanding her ten-year-old, who also spoke in code, a teenager's code. Luna was very mature for a ten-year-old and she often amazed her mother with the intellect that flowed out of her young brain. She was a child who could debate anything with any-one who was willing to listen. Luna had also become a rambunctious child on the verge of becoming a teenager and wouldn't hesitate to tell anybody anything she had on her mind. Karen tried to keep the reins tight on Luna because there were dangers out there for kids that Karen feared, especially with a free-spirited child who was con-vinced she knew everything she needed to know.

That's when Karen met Skip, who was a twenty-five-year-old surfer, and the best part of that was he spoke surfer language, which Karen wasn't too familiar with. So Luna and Skip bonded almost im-mediately. They would sit for hours and talk curls, tubes, cuts, wax, boards and other surfing topics. Oftentimes Karen would fall asleep on the couch because she had a long day at work. But she was re-lieved that she now had someone who could watch over her child in an arena that Karen was both too unfamiliar with and too busy to participate in. As a single parent Karen wanted so desperately to connect with her daughter, and even though this wasn't really con-necting mother to daughter, it was making a step forward.

CHAPTER 10

It was May on Hudson Bay, and Ursa had just stolen another caribou Bjorn was hunting. The hunter was a little ticked off at the audacity of the animal, and he thought that he had to fight for dominance of this area. So Ursa had scored another caribou and he was struggling for survival. *Maybe I'll just help myself to his feast*, he thought.

Tracks. Tracks tell a story. That's when Bjorn decided he had to stand up to this bully. He gathered up his weapons and started reading the tracks that were easier to read than a children's book. The huge bear paw prints were as large as a snowshoe track. The bear was dragging what was left of the caribou's torso, but the rack was a hindrance. So the bear removed the caribou's head with a few large bites on the neck, which reduced the drag significantly. When Bjorn came upon the scene he was a little bit taken aback. The decapitated head, with the rack attached and eyes wide open, could have been a message, which Bjorn hesitated at and then paid no attention to.

The hunter peered west and the tracks disappeared into Harrison Canyon. This is where it got sketchy. The entrance of the canyon was only about thirty feet wide and most of that was filled with the Winisk River, which was usually frozen at this time of year.

But this year it was a flowing river, and he had wondered if it meant something significant, the warmth of this winter, totally unexpected for the Northwest Territories. That's why the bears were forced inland to hunt, and that's how he lost last week's dinner. The warrior was good at avoiding ambushes, although this was looking more and more dangerous. But if he didn't stand up to his nemesis, the bear would soon be taking control of the entire area. He knew that this was a stand he had to make and he continued to move cautiously into what appeared to be a trap. The narrow opening and the commitment it represented gave Bjorn pause.

I must be nuts to do this, but I have to draw the line in the sand even though it may be the end of days as I know them. This is also a once in a lifetime opportunity, he thought.

Bjorn clutched his heavy spear with a tight hand, which could only be characterized as a death grip. Fifty yards into the canyon beyond the point of no return the canyon made a slight left turn. That's when Bjorn was committed and continued as stealthily as he could. He was reading the tracks carefully where the bear had stopped and then the tracks disappeared. No tracks, no huge polar bear, no dead caribou.

How could that huge a bear just vanish? he wondered

He was temporarily confused and surprised. When tracking you rely on your vision. As he looked at the tracks he thought they were deeper then the others so he bent down to look closer. That's when his nose detected a rank odor, and that drew his vision upward. As he lifted his head a ledge came into view at eye level. Every cell in his body was on hyper alert, and then his eyes fell on his biggest nightmare. The huge bear was up on a rock ledge about the height of the hunter's eyes. He thought that he had most certainly committed suicide. When his gaze continued down the bear's back to its face, he beheld the strangest sight.

The bear was asleep, with its head resting on the corpse of the caribou. Its face was covered in red from the caribou's blood and a slight breeze brought a rank odor to Bjorn's nostrils. His body was so tense he had to force himself not to quiver.

The bear had managed to leap from the ground to the ledge with at least forty pounds of caribou in his mouth, an astounding feat by anyone's standard. Bjorn was frozen in a combination of disbelief and fear. Then the third most incredible thing happened. The bear opened its eyes! As it beheld the scene in front of it, its nose was twitching as it took all the information in that it could. Bjorn tried not to look eye to eye at the bear. However a glance at the bear shocked Bjorn the most, because the huge and very tough animal looked . . . it looked sad. There was no anger or panic in this animal's demeanor, instead it was relaxed and calm and he actually looked sad. Bjorn wasn't sure what to do next; he was ready to sprint at a moment's notice. Then the fourth astounding event of the day occurred. The bear dozed off again. The human was still afraid to ruin the moment, and as he had been trained, he moved only his eyes to inspect his surroundings.

Bjorn had lost count of incredible events. So when he spotted the bones, he couldn't help but shake his head in disbelief as he took in the full one hundred and eighty degree view of death. He saw bones scattered around him on the ground, from many different animals. Then he saw the distinctive shape of a bear skull.

So this is a bear graveyard. Certain animals do choose a place to die, like elephants when generation after generation come to the same place, like a cemetery, Bjorn thought. The hunter realized he was courting disaster and slowly eased himself back down the trail that he had come in on. He walked back to his cabin and told Sarah the amazing story. And with the astonishing events of the day he couldn't sleep; it must have been the adrenaline still coursing through his veins.

Sarah didn't know what to make of his story and was still very skeptical of Bjorn's friendship and attachment with this creature. She still kept her distance from the bear and the animal respected that. Bjorn had heard stories of polar bears that would play with sled dogs and even befriend people. However, there were many stories of things going the other way, too. So Bjorn kept his eyes open as much as possible whenever he was around the massive bear. And slowly but surely they became hunting partners. He learned to leave a little bit for Ursa, usually the gut pile and a little meat. He rarely turned his back on the animal and always respected Ursa's territory. For example, he hardly ever walked back down into that graveyard that Ursa hung out in. He just felt it was a sacred place and he didn't want to leave tracks going into that area, so he avoided it in fear that someone else might stumble into the canyon.

CHAPTER 1 1

Sarah instantly transformed Bjorn's life, everything from a woman's voice around the cabin, to flowers gracing the table, to better meals. Bjorn's hunting skills kept them well fed, but Sarah was suspicious of Ursa, the huge polar bear. And it took a long time for each of them to get used to the other one.

With Sarah in his life, things were beginning to look up for Bjorn. Someone to help with all the work, and, of course, all the benefits that lovers shared. Sarah was amazed at Bjorn's skill with a woman's body. She thought that living up here in isolation she would have to teach him everything. However, she learned quite a lot from Bjorn about her own body.

He had a magic touch and just that touch was enough to send tingling through her entire body. After years of healing Bjorn's skin was like dried leather, instead of the melted plastic that it had looked like before. It made him appear older than his twenty-eight years, especially his left eye that drooped a little. She was sad about his burns because any attempt she made of caressing his skin was lost because the nerves in his skin were damaged. This disfigurement brought them closer together because if he had been the perfect specimen of a man, she might have felt inadequate. But Sarah's port wine stain was accepted by Bjorn and that made them a perfect pair; neither of them were judgmental, because the physical imperfections helped them bond.

About a year after they started living together, she noticed a change in her body. They had just gotten up and started breakfast.

"Are you okay?" Bjorn asked.

"Yeah, I think I must have eaten something a little rotten, my stomach has been doing somersaults," Sarah replied.

"Is that all, do you have nausea?"

"Yeah a little bit."

"Have you noticed anything else?

"Yes, Doctor Tillson, what's your diagnosis?"

"Well, you need to give me the rest of your symptoms."

"I've had this happen before and it was nothing, but I've missed my period, I don't know maybe a month or two."

"Are you pregnant?" Bjorn said with his eyes bright, "And why didn't you tell me this was going on?"

"I better not be," she said, "I've had this happen before and eventually it returns."

"Are you kidding, it would be so exciting!"

"Yeah, for you, but you don't have to walk around with a bowling ball in your gut."

"You're right. I'm being insensitive," He said with a slight smirk that was always a bit misshapen from his burns.

"Besides, we've been doing the rhythm method."

"I ain't got no rhythm."

"Obviously."

"Well, I for one am excited!"

"But this is not what I wanted."

"You have a little life inside you."

"Little, have you looked at my belly lately, I probably have a T-Rex gestating inside me."

"I'm here with you and I'm not going anywhere."

"I know, but with winter coming on, this is a difficult time."

"But, Sarah, this is the natural progression of life."

"I know and I love you and I am very excited to have our child, but this is such a difficult place to survive. I'm going to have to learn a whole new set of skills."

"And you have me, I've got a few skills, too."

"I know, Bjorn," she said as she walked over and hugged him as the tears welled up in her eyes.

"Are you okay?" he asked.

"Yes, I just have felt like I have had to puke for the last three days."

"Anything you need, you just let me know.'

The following nine months she kept getting bigger and moving slower, and she couldn't get around that easily. But Sarah kept busy with cooking and making things for the coming child. She made clothing and a papoose, but not the kind that gave the Flathead Indians their distinctive craniums. She was still very cautious around the polar bear that Bjorn had named Ursa, and who occasionally was seen around the cabin. Sarah was even worried that Bjorn was a little too trusting of this wild animal. The bear seemed to realize there was something different going on.

Bjorn only saw Ursa on occasion and feared that he would become a statistic on the Boone and Crocket list. As the winters got warmer, the bear would head inland to feed his ravenous hunger. Bjorn only saw him in the spring or fall, and now during May as the caribou herd headed north to the calving grounds. He was surprised to see the huge tracks and it was obvious that Ursa was dragging something. And Bjorn said an explicative because the bear was a much more successful hunter than he was.

The polar bear was a born predator, and with the warmer winters that they had been having, Ursa was forced to hunt ashore. But after the confrontation that Bjorn had with the bear he felt connected to the animal, however, with a child on the way he had become more cautious. Sarah had noticed that Bjorn was hesitant to turn his back on the huge animal. And now that he was the father of a coming child, he was much more cautious and asked Sarah not to wander around alone. And if Ursa was around the cabin Bjorn would order him away.

"How do you communicate with that bear?" Sarah asked.

"You mean Ursa?"

"Well, are there a bunch of other polar bears you hang out with?"

"Nope, just one incredible animal, unlike any other animal I've ever known. I don't know how he understands me, I just speak."

"And he understands your words?"

"I doubt it, but the sled dogs don't understand English, yet we still speak to them and they follow our commands."

"So did you ever figure out what was happening in Harrison Canyon?"

"No, but I didn't want to violate his trust."

"But you said you saw a bear skull."

"Yes, I did, plus tons of other skeletons."

"It's all pretty amazing. Do you think the other bear was an adversary that he killed?" Sarah asked.

"Well, with the warmer weather a lot of things are coming to light that had been frozen deep down for centuries, but Akluitok from the Inuit village said that was his mate."

"Wow, how romantic, except for the death part, he doesn't want to leave his mate," Sarah lamented.

"Yeah, I would love to explore that canyon; there have to be a lot of very interesting things buried in there. But it is definitely a holy place for him."

"And that's why you don't want to invade the sanctity of the place?"

"Yes."

"And maybe that's why he trusts you so much?"

"Maybe."

When the conversation waned, Bjorn's thoughts went back to Karen. He felt very guilty for not letting her know he was alive. But with Harlan Mckenzie trying to kill him he couldn't let his real identity be known. And he thought the burns would be an impediment to their love. He was very different than he used to be, and she was probably as beautiful as she was in her younger years.

CHAPTER 12

The black sinuous road snaked its way back and forth up the volcanic mountain as it made its way to the top. The short-haired brunette was heavy on the accelerator as she made her way to work in the predawn darkness. She only slowed the red convertible as she leaned into one of the hairpin turns. Nearing the top of the mountain she entered a bank of clouds, which slowed her down to a crawl, because encountering another vehicle here would be very dicey. Then just as she reached the peak she burst through the cloud ceiling and was driving above a layer of white clouds. She gazed out at the undercast that surrounded Haleakala and saw other volcanic peaks poking through the clouds. She often had to pinch herself because of the surprises she often found in the Hawaiian Islands. Sunrise was imminent and the orange line stretched out along the horizon. There was no better commute known to humankind, and she relished it.

Karen Harner pulled into the staff parking area of the Mees Observatory. She was anxious to get started today as an astrophysicist studying solar storms. That's why she was arriving at dawn at a place that was a beehive of activity during the nighttime hours. Much of her time here she had the place to herself, with the help of Ralph, her one tech that controlled the telescope.

"Hey, Ralph," she said.

"Hi, Karen," he replied.

"Are you ready for a big day?"

"Gotta get my coffee first."

"Get me a cup, too."

Even though she struggled with the many years she spent in school and often thought she was wasting her time with a study that was pointless and wouldn't mean anything to anyone, Karen had written her PhD thesis on coronal mass ejections and their effects on communications on Earth and in orbit. Much of her research was considered questionable during the early 1980s when she was at the University of Colorado in Boulder. However, after her thesis was complete, she moved to Tucson, Arizona, to work with her mentor J. L. Chen, who was a great inspiration to her as she negotiated the minefields of higher education. In Tucson she worked at the Kitt Peak Observatory. Then in 1980 she got a job at Mees Observatory and she started doing groundbreaking solar research. The weather wasn't half bad either. Then finally one day while she was working at Mees, all the work she had put into this unknown study was suddenly on everyone's mind.

But life wasn't all roses for Karen with two mouths to feed and all her school debts. Her father was on the same ship as Bjorn's father, and when it went down, they both died along with the rest of the crew. That's when Bjorn and Karen bonded early on; he was a senior, she was a junior. Then Bjorn left her for some crazy dream and she never saw him again, a pain she never got over. Despite a lot of dates she clung to the idea that Bjorn was her one and only.

But eventually she made it to the peak figuratively and literally. She was at the top of her profession, and finally working at Mees, a world-class observatory. But there was still a hole in her heart that even the highest level of her work couldn't fill.

Coronal mass ejections were very violent solar storms. And that's what Karen had been observing in the days prior to this; she had come up with a way to predict solar storms. But now she had proof that these storms had potential for mass destruction

"Here you go," Ralph said, handing the cup to Karen.

"Thanks," Karen said.

"So whatta we got?"

"I've been watching the signs, and if I'm right a huge CME could be brewing, so it's going to be a crazy busy day."

"Great day for a hangover!" he chuckled.

"Get some coffee and don't let me down, Ralph."

Karen was sure that some events in the past were caused by the solar storms and the powerful blasts of radiation that accompanied a CME. She had done extensive research on satellites that had come down over the years. She was certain that more dangerous and deadly solar events were coming in the future. That's why Karen was desperately trying to prove her prediction theory.

Some people in the scientific community were still denying any connection between solar activity and satellites coming down. The offered government explanation was that these satellites had deteriorated to a point that they couldn't maintain their positions, causing them to drop out of orbit and crash to Earth. However, Karen's research had dug up evidence that the problem in space was being covered up by the political party currently in power. They had scientists on staff who were discrediting Karen's work.

"Ralph, my reputation is on the line today, so shake off your alcoholic haze and get these coordinates in," Karen said as she handed him a piece of paper.

"Yes, ma'am," Ralph said with a slight salute and a smile.

The huge telescope started moving with the mechanical whirring sounds that accompany gears in motion. This was the first thing that needed to occur, before anyone could look at anything.

Karen had been extremely successful in solar astronomy. She had written her thesis on why solar storms are damaging to orbiting space craft. And the political fallout from her thesis came hard on the young college graduate student. The United States had launched Skylab in 1973; the government's position was that Skylab was still in orbit and even though there were problems during the launch things were starting to look up, and political entities in office at the time vehemently disagreed with Karen's research. Karen's mentor J. L. Chen, came to her defense. Dr. Chen was the foremost expert on solar storms and guided Karen through her advanced degrees.

The solar astronomer finished her PhD program at Taos, and then got a job at the Mees Solar Observatory on the island of Maui. She couldn't believe the luck, a great job in the most spectacular place on Earth. Karen had worked her way through the difficulties of single motherhood and the challenges of the male-dominated world of solar astronomy. And even though she never wanted this disaster to occur, it was redemption for all the hard work and struggles she had lived through. It was 1989 and Luna was twenty-one and had become a champion surfer. About a week ago Karen and Luna were sitting in the house and had a heart to heart talk, which brought them both to tears.

"Mom, I've been having the same dream for a week now."

"Tell me about your dream, Luna."

"It's a dream where I'm sitting in the woods and this bear comes up to me and stares at me."

"Were you afraid?"

"I'm terrified, but the bear turns out to be a kind bear."

Karen tried to hold back tears from her eyes. "You know your father's name was Bjorn. Do you know what Bjorn means in Scandinavian?"

"No," Luna said.

"It means bear." Karen said taking a deep breathe to compose herself. "And your father had been well named because he was a very tough bear of a man."

"Then why did he die?"

"I don't know. The army doesn't always release all the information to people who aren't in his family."

"But he's my father, isn't that family?"

"Yes, but I wasn't really related to your dad because we were never married. And I think he was in some kind of secret agency in the war, so the information on those guys was even harder to come by."

"Yeah, but don't I have any rights?"

"Yes, sweetie, so if you want to get into this I would encourage you to do it."

Karen blinked away tears and put her hands on the twenty-one-year-old's shoulders. As she looked into Luna's light blue eyes, she knew exactly where the young girl had come from.

So Clyde isn't my dad?"

"Well, it's complicated, but you are old enough to know the facts now. Clyde is your stepdad, I met him after your dad died. Clyde helped me raise you, but he is not your father," Karen said with a lifting tilt to her voice, trying to put a positive spin to a difficult topic.

"Where did Clyde go?"

"Your stepdad and I decided we couldn't live together anymore, so he got a job in California, and I got a job here in Hawaii."

"It's okay, Mom, Cindy's parents got a divorce, too, everybody does it."

"So what are you doing today?"

"I'm going surfing with Cindy."

"Do you have any homework?"

"Mom, I'm twenty-one. I'm not a child anymore, and the semester is almost over."

"Actually, you will always be MY child, so get used to it, Miss Grown Up.

CHAPTER 13

It was a cold September night. Ursa could sense something and had worked his way to Bjorn and Sarah's cabin. When he got to within fifty feet of the cabin, he laid down staring at the light coming from a window. The noises coming from inside caused his ears to twitch.

Sarah woke up suddenly; a contraction was like a hot poker being shoved into her abdomen. The pain traversed to her spine and up to her solar plexus. She had a difficult time speaking because of the pain.

She grabbed Bjorn's arm and choked out his name. "Bjorn!"

"What's wrong, Sarah?" Bjorn stammered out as he woke up.

"It's time," Sarah whispered.

"Oh, shit," Bjorn yelled as he jumped out of bed. The sled dogs out in the yard were whining and barking as they heard the excitement inside the cabin and smelled and sensed the presence of a polar bear nearby.

Despite Bjorn's advanced training in everything to do with survival, he was very lacking in medicine. So he did what men have been doing for centuries.

"I'll boil some water," he said.

"Okay, honey," Sarah said, knowing that was a task midwives gave husbands to keep them out of the way.

The contractions started at 3:00 a.m. At 3:00 a.m. the next night, the contractions were still coming, lasting about five minutes. Twenty-four hours of contractions totally consumed Sarah. The water had all boiled away and now the empty pot sat there, waiting for its next task.

Finally Sarah's water broke in a furious flush of liquid on the floor. She got up and walked around to try and move this birth along. She was bleeding slightly but consistently for the entire twenty-four hours. She used rags worn like a diaper as a sanitary napkin, because up in the Northwest Territories feminine products were hard to come by. Throughout the night the rags became saturated and then she would switch to a clean one and they began to pile up. Finally Sarah just lay down on the edge of the bed and let the blood trickle down into a pan.

Bjorn had dozed off when a slight scream from Sarah jolted him back to wakefulness.

"It's happening," Sarah said as she reached down and felt a tiny cranium between her legs.

"Okay, tell me what to do," Bjorn said.

"I don't know what to do, I thought this happened naturally."

Bjorn wasn't sure if he could touch the infant, so he just held his hands there like a catcher's mitt. Sarah pushed as hard as she could, her energy totally sapped. Bjorn was between her legs totally focused on the infant, so he didn't notice that Sarah had gotten very pale.

"I'm cold," Sarah said for the fifth time and Bjorn dug up another blanket. Suddenly he had a slimy, bloody child in his hands. He almost dropped the child and in his attempts to stop the child from hitting the floor, he smacked the soles of its feet.

"Whaaaaaa!" the child screamed.

That was the best sound Bjorn could have heard at that time. For the first time since the pain of his burn, the veteran solider felt tears draining down his face. This time they were tears of joy.

"I'm thirsty," Sarah muttered, barely audible.

Thirsty, thirsty, Bjorn thought. *That's the last thing I would be worried about now.*

He jumped up and set the child on Sarah's chest and ran to get a cup of water.

"Whaaaaa!" the child belted out, but got no response from Sarah.

"Here you go, Sarah," she reached up and grasped the cup and then dropped it on the floor.

Then the incredibly gifted fighter was in the fight of his life, with an unknown enemy that had snuck up on him. The child was turning blue and he quickly wrapped it up in one of the blankets.

"Sarah, take the child and keep it next to your body."

Sarah did not respond. Bjorn slid up beside her with the child in one arm. He slid the other arm under her torso and shook her gently.

"Sarah," he screamed.

A scream of such volume that all the dogs and the polar bear froze with their heads up, waiting for whatever was coming next."Whaaaaa!" the child screamed back.

"SARAH, don't you leave me here with this child!"

Then as if it wasn't hard enough, the warrior's life got harder then he could ever have imagined. Sarah's abdomen contracted one last time and he saw another cranium crowning and then the second child slid out on to the floor.

"What the hell is going on?" he yelled.

"Sarah, please don't go, don't leave me with these babies!" he screamed. For a trained assassin who was responsible for the deaths of at least ten people, he was shocked at the wave of emotions which swept over him. The tears were full on sobs now.

Shortly after the second child was born, a large gelatinous blood clot, as large as the second child, was passed and sat on the floor.

"Whaaaaaaa! Whaaaaa!" the infants screamed and Bjorn clicked into his action mode, thinking fast and moving even faster. He put the infants on Sarah's chest and they suckled the colostrum from her full milk glands. This calmed the babies down a bit but did nothing for the shocked dad. He realized that they were nursing from their dead mother. He put his bloody hands up to his forehead and ran his outstretched fingers down his face and released a huge sigh. This left eight blood streaks down his face, but he was too much out of his world of control to notice.

He checked her pulse just to make sure, but couldn't find a pulse anywhere. The milk from Sarah was still warm enough to satisfy the infants. The dogs in the dog yard were whining because of the excitement inside, but also because Ursa had walked up to the door of the cabin and could smell death. But he also smelled new life and he would imprint those odors in his memory.

Then Bjorn collapsed from utter fatigue and stress; he dropped down unto the bed. When he woke up to the dual wails, he rolled over and saw the big Bowie knife that he had used to cut the umbilical cords. For a second he thought he could take himself out of this nightmare. He felt a wave of depression sweep over him. He could shove that Bowie knife into his carotid arteries. It would hurt for a second but he would bleed out quickly and it would be over. He walked over and picked the knife up and raised it up to his throat. As he did his gaze went down to the floor and all the blood.

"Look, Karen, the sky is bleeding. Karen why did you leave me?" Then he shook is head and dropped the knife and it stuck in the wooden floor. Get it through your head Karen is gone and now Sarah is gone. This is true karma, he thought.

"Whaaaaaa! Whaaaaaaa!" the infants brought him back to reality. The incredibly skilled warrior felt that he had let down Karen many years ago and now Sarah. What had he missed that could have changed the circumstances. And what would he do now with two infants? He touched his nipples and knew that he couldn't produce milk.

That's when he had an idea. One of the sled dog bitches had just given birth to a litter of puppies. Bjorn walked out to the dog yard and picked up as many pups as he could. The bitch was very nervous as he walked away with the puppies. She followed him to the door of the cabin. Then he returned and scooped up the rest of the litter. He knew she would go anywhere her brood went.

Once inside he closed the door and the mother circled up her litter and lay down so they could nurse. Bjorn carried the infants over one at a time and laid them down amongst the squirming fur balls. That brought a very curious look from the female sled dog and she sniffed the babies and then licked them clean. It took awhile but eventually each child latched onto a nipple and suckled.

"Whew," Bjorn sighed. Dodged another bullet.

But he knew this wouldn't last too long and began to hatch another plan. He suddenly smiled as he gazed down at his two boys. *I've just created Romulus and Remus, the feral children,* he thought.

CHAPTER 14

It turned out that the names Romulus and Remus stuck, and as Bjorn was cleaning up the children after the birth, he noticed a curious thing on one of the children. The child that was named Romulus appeared to have several bruises on his back. However, after cleaning Romulus, and after a few days, he found the bruises didn't fade.

Bjorn realized that the marks on Romy's back were birthmarks, very much like his mother's but not as extensive. Romy's port wine stain consisted of three circles. The first started on his left shoulder and was the size of a quarter. The second circle was in the center of his back and the third one over his right rib cage, each one a little larger than the last. It had the appearance of a falling comet, and after a few days had a purple coloration like his mother's birthmark.

The new father had to make a decision after the boys were rejected by the female sled dog that was nursing them. But mostly it was the pups that were fighting with the twins over the nipples and the boys were getting scratched.

He packed the children into two papooses, kept them under his parka and then mushed to the Inuit village. The Inuit village was seven miles north of Bjorn and Sarah's cabin. As he approached the village he had to wipe away tears from his eyes. He was being forced to give up the only members of his family that were left. He had friends here; they were bonded by the challenge of survival in this harsh and foreboding land. It took him a while to get the nerve up to ask the question. It was devastating news that he had to deliver and a difficult request that he had to ask.

He went to the chief of the village and told him of the tragedy.

"Akluitok, I have no milk for the children. They will not survive unless they have milk."

The chief called together the village council. They discussed his request for almost an hour and then brought Bjorn into the ceremonial lodge. Akluitok summoned Aga, who was a woman who had just lost a child. The Inuits could not pronounce Bjorn's name and they called him Akycha, which is Sun God in Inuit. They called him Sun God because it looked like he had been burned by the Sun.

"Akycha, our hearts go out to you," Akluitok said, "What you ask will be a great burden on our village."

"I will pay your village, great chief," Bjorn said.

"What do you offer, Sun God?' Akluituk said.

"You may have my sled and most of my dog team," Bjorn said, "I will not need them anymore."

The council discussed this great gift.

Then the chief stood up and said. "Akycha, this is a generous gift, we accept your offer."

"Thank you, Akluitok."

"This is Aga, she has lost her child."

"Aga, I thank you for your kindness," Bjorn said.

The young woman nodded.

The chief translated to Aga as Bjorn spoke. "I will leave the boys here until they are past the nursing phase," Bjorn said, the chief nodded, knowing the need for a quiet hunt. "And when I hunt I will bring you meat for the boys, when they get to the phase where they eat meat, until that time I will bring food for you." Bjorn didn't like leaving his sons, but he knew he was not fit to care for the infants.

"Thank you, Aga."

Aga nodded again.

Bjorn left with a heavy heart. But he knew that this was the best choice, if the babies were to survive. And maybe it would help Aga deal with the loss of her child.

When the hunter returned to the cabin, he was amazed to see Ursa lying on the porch of the place. He had left with a full dog team, but returned with only two dogs pulling him on skis. Skijoring, as the Scandinavians called it, was a very efficient way to travel. The sled dog called Wing Nut was a wheel dog and he was the power of this operation. Wheel dogs had a lot of strength and were often harnessed right in front of the sled. Without the weight of a fully loaded sled, Wing Nut and Cooper, a lead dog, could get Bjorn moving at almost twenty miles per hour.

Once the dogs were secured in their beds, Bjorn did something that he didn't think he would ever do. But at this point he had nothing to lose; the boys were taken care off, Sarah was gone and he had given most of the dogs away. Ursa had that sad look he had when he first met him in Harrison Canyon. Bjorn really didn't care if this huge bear took him out; he had lost everything.

He approached Ursa and scratched the bear behind the ears. The two sled dogs watched in earnest, tilting their heads to the side as they observed what could be the end of their alpha male. But Ursa just leaned his big head back, enjoying the feeling. When Bjorn finished the rub down, the huge bear opened his eyes, as if in appreciation. Then he walked away from the bear and approached the cabin door to do a task that could be the hardest thing he had ever done.

The door swung open and Bjorn saw the body on the floor with a blanket covering it. Dried blood that had seeped out from under the blanket was all around the body. A foul odor of death hung heavy in the air. He felt he had failed the woman that put so much responsibility on him and he was supposed to know how to survive, but he had failed her. The next thing that he did was gather up the things he needed to live off the land and took them out to load on the small sled. He would have to make several trips to accomplish this with the smaller sled.

Then he stacked firewood around Sarah's body. He didn't uncover her body because he wanted to remember her as the vibrant person he had known. The final task was the match. The wood caught fire quickly. As Bjorn walked out, he had an uncomfortable feeling under his skin which he felt every time he was near fire now. Cremation was an acceptable from of disposing of a body in many cultures, and Bjorn had no problem with it. He wasn't a praying man, but he said a few quick words and they were mostly apologizing for failing her. Then the hardened man stepped back and shook his head. He looked at Ursa and said, "Go, Ursa."

He walked down off of the porch and turned around one last time to watch his home and his lover go up in smoke. Then he packed the sled and harnessed the dogs. Since he only had two dogs left it took them five trips to haul everything. Then his life officially changed. The distance to Harrison Canyon and his new life was short.

CHAPTER 15

Twelve years after Karen and Luna settled on Maui, Karen was the director of the day shift activities at the Mees Observatory. Her work was widely accepted now and her detractors were minimal.

Luna worked part-time in a pizza shop and surfed full-time. She had won national titles and often traveled to sites around the world to surf. At age twenty-one she had developed into a gorgeous woman and broke a lot of hearts. The last twelve years had been tough for Karen. Just to get Luna through high school was a challenge because she wanted to surf her way through.

Karen was very excited because it was the eleventh year of the coronal cycle, and large solar storms typically showed up every eleven years. It had been eleven years since the last coronal mass ejection in 1978. If she was right this could be the year of the next big solar display and she had been gearing up for this event all year.

The solar weather had been giving signals to Karen all year but she didn't know when the event was going to happen. She was putting in twelve-hour days because she had to be there during the solar hours and then several hours after the sunset to study the images that had been received during the day.

It was Thursday, March 9, when all hell broke loose. At 2:00 a.m. Karen was awakened by the telephone ringing. Her first thought was, *Where is Luna?* But she remembered Luna was back in Maui, she was still a little uneasy because she knew that Luna was at her boyfriend's house. They had both returned from a surfing competition just the day before. Anytime she got a call at 2:00 a.m. she held her breath.

"Hello?" she said with a questioning tone.

"Hi, Karen, this is Ernie Parlance."

Ernie was the director of celestial observations at the Mees Observatory and Karen only spoke with him at observatory meetings. She had very little interactions with the vampire crew and couldn't remember if she had ever gotten a nighttime call from the observatory. However, she was very happy that it wasn't a call from the hospital.

"What's up, Ernie?" Karen said rubbing her eyes.

"Sorry to bother you at such a late hour. But we are getting reports from all around the planet that we are having a wildly intense aurora borealis tonight. And I just thought you would want to know.

Wildly intense, she thought, her brain not totally online yet. Then it clicked. Finally her prediction had come true, and her research had paid off.

Karen told Ernie, "I'm on my way."

Karen knew that solar storms sent solar particles to the atmosphere of the Earth, which caused aurora borealis, and the stronger the storm the more intense the aurora.

She dropped the phone as she jumped out of bed and ran to her closet. She threw a T-shirt and a sweatshirt on and slipped into a pair of jeans. Karen made a faster trip up the mountain then she usually did. But her spirits dropped when she got to the peak and it was completely socked in with clouds. When she walked into the observatory she found Ernie.

"Hi, Ernie, thanks for the heads up."

"Sure, Karen, but I'm sure you saw that we are on hold for now, because the lens is completely obscured."

"I was worried about that. What does the forecast look like?"

"Well, it's not looking good, so since it's almost four o'clock, I've sent half my crew home."

Karen walked outside to see if she could see any openings in the cloud bank.

Shit, that's just my luck, my big chance and I won't be able to see anything, she thought.

"Hello, Miss Harner."

Karen jumped a little and spun around when see heard the deep, husky voice.

"Oh, hi, Hoku, you scared me."

Hoku was a Hawaiian security guard at the observatory and had been for the twelve years that Karen had been there. He was a perfect choice for this position because he was as big as a mountain. Yet he was very respectful and had always treated Karen like a princess from the day she began, even though a lot of the astronomers challenged her.

"You know, Hoku, you can call me Karen."

"Yes, ma'am," he said.

"So, Hoku, I really need a clear day," she said.

"Yes ma'am, you will have clear weather all day."

"Really," she said looking around at the clouds. "How do you know this, Hoku?"

"My people have been studying the weather for many generations and I have learned from my father and my grandfather."

Wow, you are kidding me, this could have helped out a lot over the past twelve years. Why didn't anyone know about this skill of yours?"

"No one asked me, Miss Karen."

"If you are right, I will buy you dinner, Hoku. Because this will make me famous."

The big man blushed and looked at the ground.

"You could be my secret weapon, Hoku."

"Yes, ma'am."

Karen turned around in a circle trying to see what he was seeing, but it looked the same as any overcast night to her. She walked back inside and decided to bet the farm on this hunch. She went to her office. Now she had to decide on the biggest risk of all, which coordinates she should put in to see the best view of the CME. Then she had a blinding glimpse of the obvious. Actually, it wasn't obvious, but it was right in front of her face if she would just accept it. There were a lot of reports coming in from around the globe about an impending solar storm.

I wonder if Hoku can tell me anything about this predicted CME? Can he read any signs that indicate there may be a solar storm coming? she thought. Then she walked outside and ran into another security guard.

"Where is Hoku?"

"I'm sorry, ma'am, he just punched out."

Karen looked up and saw the taillights at the front gate. She ran at full speed to the front gate and yelled, "Hoku!"

The brake lights suddenly flashed on. When she caught up to the car, she was out of breath.

"Hoku . . . I have another . . . question for you."

"Yes, ma'am," Hoku replied.

"Do your people know . . . if the Sun is going to have . . . a big storm on it?"

Hoku looked up at the moon barely visible through the thin cloud layer. "Yes, ma'am, very big storm on the Sun today."

Karen's jaw dropped open. She had been studying this for fifteen years and here these ancient people had all the answers.

"Is your big telescope not working?"

"No, it's working fine. But you and your people know all this, already."

"My people have been worshiping the Sun since my people have been here. We worship Mother Earth and Father Sun."

Karen stood there in stunned silence. Hoku looked at her like she was crazy.

"Okay, Hoku, you have a great day off, and thank you for you help."

"Yes, ma'am."

Karen shook her head in disbelief.

All this equipment and money and time, and this ancient civilization already knows all this. Why do we have to reinvent the wheel every couple of hundred years? Karen thought.

The next thing Karen did was call Ralph.

"Hi, Ralph, this is Karen," she said.

"Oh, not again," he said.

"Yeah, Ralph, this is going to be a very big day."

"That's what you said the last time, and I had a hangover all day."

"Well, whose fault was that?"

"You didn't make it any easier on me!"

"Come on, Ralph, I have it on good authority that this will be the day."

"Whose authority?"

"Hoku."

"Hoku? Hoku, the security guard!"

"Yup!"

"Is this a joke?"

"Nope."

"Okay, I'll try to be there in the next hour."

"How about the next half hour."

The phone clicked off as Ralph lost patience with the phone call, and slammed the receiver down.

Then she called her mentor, J. L. Chen. He had just gotten to work.

"Hi, Doctor Chen, this is Karen Harner."

"Don't you mean Doctor Harner? You must be very busy."

"Yes, I am," she said.

"I spent the last night looking at a faint aurora. Way down here in New Mexico."

"Are you kidding me?"

"No, that's a first for me, but rumors are that you will be able to see it in Hawaii before it's all over."

"No way."

"Oh yes, this is your time to shine, Karen."

"Doctor Chen, did you know that the Hawaiian people can predict the weather and even when a solar storm is coming."

"Yes, I have studied the Hawaiian and Samoan cultures for years. How do you think I did all my research?"

This was a morning of being shocked and Karen sat there stunned again, like she was the last one to be told a secret.

"Well, Doctor Chen, I don't know what to say, I'm amazed."

"Don't be, now that you know my secret, you should tap into the ancient cultures in all of the South Pacific."

"Yes, I mean no, I mean I'm a little busy with this upcoming event, but yes I will research this knowledge."

"Karen, I'm going to be at the conference for solar storms in Albany, New York. Aren't you going to be there?"

"You know with this approaching CME, I'm not sure I can miss this."

"Indeed Karen, and the other thing you need to do is contact the scientific advisor for the administration and let them know we have this CME coming."

"Yes, I have that on my to do list."

"Okay, Dr. Harner, I will see you in Albany if you make it," Dr. Chen said. Karen still wasn't used to that title and she blushed a little to hear her mentor refer to her as doctor.

"Yes, I'm leaving tomorrow to start the ten-hour flight."

The next call Karen made was to the White House switchboard, and asked for the scientific advisor for the administration. It took about ten minutes to be connected, and eventually Jay Riley came on the line. It was 11:00 a.m. in Washington.

"Hello?" Riley said.

"Hello, Dr. Riley, this is Dr. Karen Harner. I am a solar astrophysicist at Mees Observatory in Maui, Hawaii."

"How's the weather out there, Dr. Harner?"

The weather was always the first topic of discussion anytime anyone from the mainland was on the phone. And Karen's mind went back to the conversation she just had with Hoku.

"The weather is always perfect here." Karen replied.

"Oh, I'm so jealous of you, but I guess that's why your observatory is in Hawaii."

"Yes, sir. The reason I'm calling is because the Earth may possibly be hit with an enormous solar storm and this could seriously affect the power grid and satellites orbiting the planet. Worst case scenario it could change life as we know it."

Suddenly Dr. Riley was less jovial. "And when will this occur, Dr. Harner?"

"It's still dark in Hawaii, but I will have a good idea of the timeline when I get a look at the Sun in a few hours. If it is a big storm it will probably take several days to get here," she said.

"Okay, I will inform the people who need to know. Keep me updated."

Karen knew that calls to the White House were always recorded, but she had kept her composure.

CHAPTER 16

It was March of 1989. Four years earlier, Bjorn had returned to the Inuit village to get his boys back. It was a difficult thing to do because even though he had visited often, it was like he was an uncle. Remus had started to notice a resemblance to his father. With a lot of explanation he eventually took both of them to Harrison Canyon, where he had been living in a wall tent and following a subsistence living. The boys were ten at the time and it had been a strain on Aga but with the help of the village and Bjorn, they made it.

However, Romy's development was delayed because his words were always garbled, like he was trying to speak with a rag in his mouth. Out of frustration, Aga taught him to communicate by making clicks with his tongue and then added more sounds that he could make with his cheeks and throat. Eventually they created a myriad of words to communicate with. He only had about a hundred words but combined with gestures he got the message across.

While Romy was in Harrison Canyon the one that he communicated the best with was Ursa. After a brief time so that they could get used to each other, they became best friends. Ursa somehow seemed to understand the clicks and whirs better than anyone. It also seemed that Ursa knew the boys' scent from a long time ago.

One day when Bjorn walked out of the wall tent, to his extreme consternation he saw that Romy had climbed up on Ursa's back and was attempting to ride the bear like a horse. Romy was having a great time but Bjorn almost lost his breakfast and Ursa seemed confused by the incident. Romy was clicking and whirring like he was having the best day of his life. Bjorn kept his cool and talked Romy into sliding down off of the bear's back. Bjorn proceeded to scold the boy for what he thought was a very foolish act that could have gotten him killed.

It was very arduous on Bjorn because he couldn't talk to Romy and all of their hunts had been unsuccessful due to his inability to learn the language. Bjorn could not understand the language they had developed for Romy and had to rely on rudimentary sign language.

Bjorn thought it was time to teach the boys to hunt. But there was something wrong with Romy, at least he had developed differently than Remus. Romy was very slow and his speech was an insurmountable challenge. With the broad short skull and slanted eyes it was a well-known syndrome, but no one in the Northwest Territories recognized these signs. But they all knew he was different than Remus, who had become a strapping warrior type like his father and a protégé when it came to survival and hunting.

Romy loved to explore Harrison Canyon, and often came back with rocks and leaves that caught his eye; one day he took an interest in an old weathered log. He came back to the camp and tried talking to Bjorn.

"Click, click, umpf, whir, click, click," Romy said.

Bjorn stared at him, trying to understand, but was lost. Then Remus, who had been raised with Romy, spoke up.

"He's saying he saw something," Remus said.

"What did you see, Romy?" Bjorn asked.

"Whir, whir, click . . . umpt, whir," Romy said. As he pointed up the canyon. Bjorn just looked at Remus, asking for translation.

"I think he's saying he found a log," Remus said.

"Well, there are logs all over the place," Bjorn said. Remus just shrugged his shoulders. By now Romy was pointing wildly into the canyon.

"Click, click, umpf."

"Okay, let's see your log," Bjorn said, as he rolled his eyes.

As they walked away from the camp, the sled dogs whined in anticipation of going on a trip. About a quarter of a mile into the canyon, the searchers stopped and the guide seemed a little confused. Romy looked around as if trying to remember where he was and where the log was.

"Let's go, this was just another wild goose chase," Remus said.

"Oh, oh, umpf, whir," Romy said as he suddenly remembered. And then he ran twenty feet and stood there gazing down at the riverbank that had been freshly cut by the Winisk River. Romy stood there pointing with a look of triumph on his face. As Bjorn and Remus got up to him, they saw a white loglike object protruding out of the river bank. The really odd part of the log was that it tapered to a point at the end.

"Oh my God," Bjorn exclaimed, "That's a tusk, that's a huge tusk, it's like a mammoth tusk!" It was the moment that Bjorn suddenly realized that Romy's difficulties were with his speech alone, and he had a level of intelligence that may be different than Remus, but was still there. He wondered if Romy or Aga had invented the language that he used. That's when Bjorn made it his goal to learn Romy's style of communication.

"Click, click, whir, umpf, umpf," Romy said with a wide grin and gesticulating.

"He wants to dig it up," Remus said with some excitement in his voice. "Can we, Dad?"

"Of course, let's go get a shovel."

When they returned with the needed tools, Ursa was sniffing the tusk.

"Well, now we know why Ursa stands guard over this place, this is a cemetery!" Bjorn said.

Even though the weather had been a lot warmer, the ground was still frozen and the work proceeded at a snail's pace. But as the pick landed once near the tusk, something caught Bjorn's eye. He called a halt to the work and jumped down into the creek. As he studied the bank he saw a lot of glistening bits, and that's when he caught a glimpse of the mother of all nuggets. It was about half the size of a golf ball and he picked it up and rinsed it off in the creek. He felt his heart pounding.

"What is it, Dad?"

"Oh, just a pretty stone."

Soon after that find, Romy grew homesick and left to return to the village. Bjorn followed him but at a distance to see if he could make the right decisions. The boy, even though a little slow, managed to make it back to the village. Aga took him in. Bjorn came into the village and had a long talk with Aga, and they both agreed this would be the best solution for everyone involved because Romy was much more comfortable with Aga. She was lonely after the boys left, and Bjorn was concerned that Romy needed someone who could understand him. This turned out to be the perfect arrangement for everyone, because Romy was happy, Aga was happy and Bjorn was relieved.

Bjorn and Remus had gotten very good at survival, almost as good as the Inuit hunters and they supplied the village with meat to help pay for Romy's care. But most importantly they clicked with this land and were home there. Remus learned how to make every weapon that could be created in the wilderness. Throwing sticks, bows, arrows, spears, spear throwers, the list was endless. At first Bjorn was Remus's protege with weapons, but eventually Remus got better than his father. He was the one that made the spear thrower which was called an atlatl, an ancient device that increased the range of a lightweight spear by three times. The father and son often sat and talked about every detail to improve their hunting. Since they didn't have guns they needed to develop their skills with ancient weapons to perfection. Remus even became very proficient at knapping flint, a skill that took patience, strength and an eye to see the finished product in a chunk of stone.

When he was in Churchill, Manitoba, on the southwest shore of Hudson Bay, he would find old leaf springs from a car suspension, to make into knife blades. Still, he preferred flint and would spend a lot of time into the late hours working the stone. Winter was the best time to knap the flint. Remus would use a harder rock to chip off a piece of flint, and then he would use the tine of a caribou antler to finish the point. It was a huge source of pride for the boy and for his father as well. Bjorn visited Romy and Aga whenever he delivered meat to the village.

Churchill was a major polar bear viewing area with tundra buggies, allowing normal tourists to view the bears. Bjorn was concerned about this because if anyone got a glimpse of Ursa, there would be endless tours into their area to see the massive creature. And worse case scenario, a hunter would show up to claim this prize.

Then March 9th came. That night Bjorn climbed out of his sleeping bag to urinate. He could tell that something was not quite right; the tent was a strange color. When he walked out it was like there was a green spotlight in his face. It was so bright that it almost seemed like daylight. As he looked around and saw Ursa, the bear was as confused by the light as anyone. The entire bear was green except his nose.

"Hey, Remus, get out here!"

There was a rustle in the tent and soon Remus came out of the tent armed to the teeth, thinking his father was being attacked.

"What the hell is this? I've never seen the northern lights this bright."

"Yeah, this is amazing."

"You know, dad, it looks like the sky is bleeding."

Bjorn stood there stunned, gazing at Remus.

"What's wrong?" Remus asked

"Nothing, just remembered something from my past," Bjorn said. *This reminds me of that night back in Michigan with Karen*, he reminisced

"Yeah, you need to tell me about your past sometime."

As they gazed skyward, they saw ribbons, curved flowing lines and what looked like rain coming down. And the strangest thing was that it was all green and unlike other nights that they saw the lights. This time there were no dark areas of the sky, the entire sky was green. Bjorn put his hands in his pockets to warm them, and that's when he realized he still had the nugget in his pocket. He knew the gold was very valuable. But he was also wise enough to realize that if the discovery of this gold got out, their lives would change beyond anything recognizable.

But unknown to either of them, their lives were about to change forever and the past was going to catch up with them.

CHAPTER 17

The weather in Moscow was atrocious. Snowstorms kept pounding the city and life for the residents was taxing. Three feet of snow piled up around the satellite monitoring office. Nikolai was the first to notice the wobble in the flight path of Cosmos 956. It was just a subtle change but to eyes accustomed to the printout of codes, it glared at him. Cosmos 954 had dropped out of orbit just 11 years before and though it was well known in history, no one from that era was left in this tracking center. The minor techs had been shipped out to other assignments while the brass of the center ended up in Siberia or worse, dead.

"What do we do now!?" Sergei asked, his eyes wide with panic.

Nikolai was calm while analyzing the printout taken from the last twenty-four hours and simultaneously creating a plan in his mind.

"You must calm down, Sergei," Nikolai mumbled while looking around. The KGB often had agents wandering around the tracking center. Nikolai walked to the front door and eased it closed. Sergei's anxiety was causing the volume of his voice to ratchet up.

"I have a wife and a child now, how can I calm down!"

"We have done nothing wrong, but we have to calmly prepare for how the government will react to this. And we need to tell the same story."

Get a hold of yourself comrade, or I will kill you myself, Nikolai thought.

"They will react the same way they did with 954! My friend Anatoly was never seen again!"

"You can't spend all your time worrying about the bad possibilities. Instead put your brain to work on fixing this problem," Nikolai said. *I know Sergei is right but I also know that when confronting a problem one cannot lose control.* Nikolai thought.

Sergei began to calm down and with a big sigh he walked over to the table where Nikolai was working and began analyzing the printouts. Soon it became apparent to both men that the orbiter had lost all power, but how and what could be done about it? Without power the satellite wasn't able to fire its thrusters and maintain a synchronous orbit. Therefore the orbit would slowly degrade until the satellite dropped out of space and fell to a fiery death on the surface of the Earth.

This was not one of the fancy satellites that the United States sent up. This was a spy satellite with just the basic equipment and minimal protection from solar radiation. But the Soviet Union depended on these birds to keep an eye on their arch enemy and nemesis in the space race. Nikolai began checking a myriad of circuits to see if he could restart the thrusters or reboot the computer. Unfortunately, it seemed like every circuit had been fried from some unknown source.

Nikolai's mind ran wild. "Perhaps the Americans have developed a weapon that can fry a satellite's circuitry," he said.

With the control of the satellite gone, it began to wobble in orbit. The wobble would eventually become so pronounced that it would break through the stratosphere and come down in a flaming ball of debris.

The door to the office swung open and a man with a shaved head and absolutely no expression on his face stood staring at the two scientists. Behind him were two thugs. Sergei inhaled audibly. That made the KGB henchman focus on him.

"What's wrong with 956?" the chrome dome blurted out. The KGB had spies in the monitoring center and one of them had detected Sergei's angst and sent the troops in.

Nikolai walked over to the computer console and began typing in nonsensical commands, knowing that the KGB agent wouldn't know a shift key from an on/off button.

"We are very busy in here right now, but if you want me to stop and talk to you, just let me know. I'm sure your commander won't mind."

"I am the commander!" the bald officer blurted out, and then seemed to be gritting his teeth. "There are two of you in here. One of you better start talking."

Wow, this guy can count, Nikolai thought. And then pointed to the console. Sergei picked up on the fabrication and walked over to the computer being blocked by the two thugs and said, "Excuse me." Then he started typing false commands into the computer.

The commander began looking around the room to see if there was anything amiss, but seeing nothing, he shouted, "You better get that bird flying again, comrades!"

Nikolai thought fast and then speaking in low tones almost whispering, he said, "We've just discovered that the satellite was damaged by something from Earth."

"What could have done that?"

"I don't know. There isn't a giant volcano going off anywhere." Then Nikolai stared at the bald KGB agent in silence. Playing this confrontation to the hilt.

"Could this be a weapon?"

Nikolai shrugged his shoulders while simultaneously giving a slight nod.

Hook, line and sinker, Nikolai thought, as the American phrase goes.

"We have no record of satellites, space debris or meteorites anywhere near our satellite. And there is no record of missiles coming anywhere near 956 in the last thirty days. But you never know, I've heard the Americans have been working on a giant laser."

The commander stormed out of the room with the two thugs in close pursuit.

CHAPTER 18

Dr Jay Riley, a scientist and now scientific advisor to President Thomas Hoaglund, had a long and distinguished career in science, starting as professor of an Ivy League university and finishing off with appointments to several administrations, most recently the administration of Thomas Hoaglund. As news from around the world started to filter into the White House, Dr. Riley started to become nervous and reached out to the secretary of the environment for help with this.

It was nearing the end of President Hoaglund's term, with the elections coming up in November. Jay Riley was a professor of chemistry but his real strength was knowledge in a variety of disciplines. Therefore, Dr. Jay Riley had more than a passing interest in medicine, and while not a medical doctor he knew a lot about the human body.

While the administration's doctor had tried hard to keep this information close to the vest, it appeared to people close to him that the president was in the early stages of dementia. Mostly it was frequent and significant memory lapses. Therefore, when Dr. Riley talked to President Hoaglund, he was very aware of the need to speak clearly and concisely. He also had never gotten used to the repetitive questioning, but considering that this was the president of the United States, he could definitely tolerate it.

Since this was a pretty advanced scientific discussion, he had to work on his presentation, so that everyone understood what the risks were. That's when he requested a meeting in the situation room with as much of the cabinet as he could get. All the secretaries were there that related to the realm of concern.

"Mr. President, there is going to be a solar event that may strongly affect the Earth," Dr Riley started. He had already briefed the secretaries of defense and environment, but none of them had the expertise to speak with any level of knowledge.

"Is it a meteorite?" the president asked as everyone in the room held their collective breath.

"Well, first, sir, meteors are falling through space, whereas meteorites have crashed into the Earth, and, no, it's not a meteor."

"Damn, that's lucky!"

"But it's something that could be very devastating to this planet, our country and our way of life."

"Go ahead, Dr. Riley," the president said.

"Sir, I've been speaking with an expert on solar storms and we are looking at a very intense solar storm called a coronal mass ejection. I am no expert on these storms, but this could be very devastating to everything that we know."

"Well, why haven't we seen anything like this before?"

"We have sir, but those were smaller storms. This storm could be an astronomically huge storm, Riley replied."

"Well, what's going to happen to us? Are we all going to get fried?"

"No, sir, but we could have problems such as satellites dropping out of orbit and a worse case scenario would be our power grid failing," Riley said.

"So it would be like that meteorite crash landing in the state down south," he said while gesturing with his index finger, which was typical of President Hoaglund.

"Arizona," someone in the room said.

"No, sir, that crater is near Winslow, Arizona, and it was the result of a meteorite impacting the Earth some fifty thousand years ago."

"How can we stop this?"

"Sir, my expertise ends at this point and I recommend we get an expert here."

"Who would that be?"

"Karen Harner, she's a world-renowned solar astrophysicist in Hawaii."

"Get her here as soon as possible."

"Yes, sir," Jay Riley said.

"In fact," the president said, looking at the secretary of defense. "Let's get her a military ride. I don't want her waiting in terminals when we could have her here a lot sooner."

"Yes, Mr. President," the secretary answered.

The meeting broke up and the president indicated he wanted to talk to the scientific advisor and the secretary of defense.

"Yes, sir," the men said simultaneously.

"Secretary Willis, since this is a matter of national security, let's get the CIA involved and get this astronomer, um . . . um." The president said snapping his fingers.

"Doctor Harner," Jay Riley responded, seeing the president struggling to remember.

"Yes, Miss Harner."

"Okay, Mr. President, I'll contact Chief Mckenzie."

"Good, and, Mr.Riley, give me a percentage on what your think the chances are for total destruction."

"That's hard to say, but this disaster will probably be in stages, if anything happens at all."

"What do you mean by stages?"

"Well, the CME will occur and then the power grid will fail and things will get worst from there. Doctor Harner has been studying this for decades and she would be the best one to get this info from."

"And what is the percentage of total destruction?"

"Mr. President, I am sorry I just don't know the answer to that."

"Really?"

"I'm sorry, Mr. President, but Miss Harner said the last CME of this size was back in 1859 and it is called the Carrington Event."

"1859 . . . I bet they got slammed back then."

"Not really, sir, they didn't have satellites and power grids to worry about back then. It was probably not even noticed with the exception of the northern lights."

"And there's no huge crater or anything?"

"Ah, no, sir, these are not meteorites," Willis and Riley glanced at each other.

"Oh, yeah, well I'm new to all this science stuff, Ripley."

At this point the scientific advisor was so frustrated that he decided to let the name change slide.

CHAPTER 19

The Akula fast attack sub slid silently through the water in Hudson Strait. The crew had orders to do an exercise in the frozen Arctic Ocean under the ice cap. The exercise was to see how long it would take the sub to get from the Atlantic to the Pacific in case a crisis erupted in the world.

They were about one hundred miles east of Killiniq Island. Before they went under the ice, Captain Zharkov would surface the Akula and receive orders. After that they would be isolated and out of communication for at least three days.

The periscope broke the surface and Captain Zharkov took the handles in both hands and slowly rotated in a three hundred and sixty degree arch. Seeing nothing in any direction except a distant freighter, he ordered the helmsman to surface and shortly the conning tower broke the surface, making a dramatic display of white ocean water falling down off the black almond-shaped conning tower. Gulls circled around the new feature in their world, making raucous calls and looking for possible sources of food.

Immediately after the tower was above the water, the radio engineer started recording an encrypted message from their base. A change of plans. The captain's right eyebrow lifted when the radio engineer walked up to him and handed him a slip of paper. The captain had a practiced look of non-interest because in the past he knew the crew around him was reading his expression.

The captain read the message and had a look of boredom as he contemplated the orders, but the next act gave everything away. He picked up his microphone and said, "Executive officer to the bridge immediately," in a baritone voice. Everyone around him was suddenly aware that this was not going to be an average day.

It was routine practice to allow as many sailors as possible to climb the ladder and stand on the conning tower. They were even allowed to climb down to the deck and walk around on top of the sub and breathe the cold salt air, even if it was only for a couple minutes. The message changed all of that and the men already on the ladder were ordered off by the XO, to a chorus of groans. The captain then ordered the hatch to be closed and the sub to dive immediately. The XO was summoned to his office to discuss the situation.

The third one in line to climb the ladder was the embodiment of pure evil. Dimitry had made it through the Afghanistan debacle. But he didn't leave that country without killing as many Afghans as he could; he was an extremely diabolical assassin. When he returned to Russia he missed the rush of killing. He started drinking heavily and in one bar fight he killed a man. Because he was a valuable asset to the Russian special forces as a very skilled sniper, the military didn't want to lose him. But they couldn't let him wander around killing civilians. Therefore the military put him in the safest place they could think of. That was on a sub, one hundred feet below the surface of the ocean. When his psychotic impulses got the best of him, Dimitry found himself chained to a steel ring on the wall of one of the steel missile tubes. That was as close to jail as they had in the sub, and he found himself there often for fighting and putting other sailors into medical.

Because of his enjoyment of seeing people suffer he actually disliked his status as a sniper; he was too far away to enjoy the pain of his victims. When the captain ordered everyone off the conning tower, Dimitry grinned. He knew this meant there may be some action coming. Unfortunately for him, being in a submarine was worse than being a sniper. Couldn't see shit. He had been on the sub for one year and he was eager to fight on land again, where he could continue his reign of terror.

Soon after the men were ordered back to their stations, the captain gave orders to swing the sub around to a westerly direction towards Hudson Bay. Within five minutes everyone was back in their positions and the sub was diving. Once fully submerged the captain gave coordinates to the helmsman and then embarked on the strangest mission any of them had ever experienced.

The Hudson Bay and its surrounding waterways had been mapped out very little. This was because if the Americans or the Canadians knew they were in this body of water they could tighten the noose. This was dangerous territory for a Russian sub because of the close relationship between the Canadians and the United States and the dead end nature of the bay. The bay had a relatively narrow entrance by Nottingham Island and a submarine could be trapped in the bay fairly easily. Russian subs weren't welcomed just anywhere, especially lurking around North America. It would be an international incident if the sub was discovered in the bay, but an important piece of Russian property was in the bay, and they had to reclaim it or destroy it.

Once they got by Mansel Island, they were a little safer cruising down the open bay as ordered. The sub cruised seventy five feet below the surface, stealthily slinking its way three hundred miles south of Churchill near the Polar Bear Provincial Park. Calculations made by the tracking office put the pending landfall of Cosmos 956 somewhere in that area, if the techs could not get it flying again.

The sub was safe now because the bay was still frozen and they would be under the ice until they decided to surface. When they arrived at a point ten miles out from the shore they continued creeping in slowly until they were at the agreed upon location and darkness had fallen. The captain ordered the helmsman to surface. It was a rapid surfacing because that was the practiced technique to beak through the ice.

The conning tower proved to be a formidable battering ram. Like someone breaking a pencil over their knee, it lifted the ice until it snapped and then it continued driving upwards through the hole it had punched. Water and huge chunks of ice fell off the conning tower, landing with a splash in the icy bay.

The most important thing now was to make radio contact with the base in the homeland.

"Captain," the radio engineer said.

Captain Zharkov spun around with his eyes glaring at the subordinate. He always got his way when they had an important mission. His crew always walked around as if they were walking on eggshells.

"A message sir," he said as he handed the paper to the captain.

Captain Zharkov continued locking eyes with the radio engineer; he enjoyed controlling people and or situations with the slightest look or word. Eventually the engineer was quivering and trying to hide his tremors as he looked away.

Zharkov kept a blank face. His mouth was a straight line, neither a smile nor a frown. Then he suddenly stretched out his arm, and the engineer made a gasp and took a step back like he was trying to get away from an imminent blow. The radio engineer blushed as other people noticed his fear.

"May I return to my station, sir?"

"No, I want you to stay here and shine my shoes," the captain sneered.

The tenseness and fear was palpable in the sub, because they were in enemy territory and their mission was unclear.

I'm glad I have Dimitry on this warship, he's the only one that won't crumble when someone says "boo," Zharkov thought.

"Get the XO in my office, and I want Dimitry and Aleksei there, too."

"Yes, sir," the first officer said, and then he called the required people.

"You have the helm."

"I have the helm," the first officer said, with a sharp salute.

Zharkov walked to the office and the XO met him there with Dimitry and Aleksei close behind. The captain addressed the small group.

"We have a situation. A Russian satellite may be coming down and the KBG thinks it will be crash landing right around here. Our job is to eliminate anyone who sees it and to destroy as much of the satellite as possible and send it to the bottom of the bay," Zharkov said.

"Might . . . be coming down?" Dimitry responded.

"They are trying to keep it flying," the captain said.

"Which means it's coming down, we just don't know when," Dimitry said

The XO and Aleksei watched the verbal sparring, and the XO for one was surprised to see anyone go face to face with the captain.

"Look, Dimitry, I got you on this boat for a scenario just like this one."

"And I didn't ask for any favors," Dimitry said.

"Are you saying you don't have the balls for this?" Zharkov asked.

"You know I have the fucking balls for this, and your wife knows it, too!" Dimitry shouted.

"So what's your problem then?"

"Floating around in this steel tube is my problem, with a bunch, with a bunch of guys that have nothing to do but jerk off for fun," Dimitry spit out.

"And what's wrong, you can't get it up?"

"Fuck you!"

The XO stood up and yelled, "You will not disrespect our captain. You will be court-martialed and end up in Siberia!"

Zharkov chuckled, looked at the XO and said, "Sit down, we go way back, and he has always broken the rules."

Dimitry's statement was the kind that could end a sailor with a burial at sea, whether the sailor wanted it or not. But with Zharkov and Dimitry there was history. They had fought side by side in Afghanistan a decade before, and it is still a debate as to whether Dimitry saved Zharkov and a lot of other Russian lives. Some sources claimed that Dimitry was a hero, while others said he was too busy killing to be saving anyone. Capitan Zharkov stayed silent on the topic and never commented.

The captain stood up and unlocked a locker and removed an AK-47 with a scope.

"There, you feeling better now?"

Then he handed the ammunition to Aleksei.

"When that satellite comes down, you and Aleksei are going to find it and eliminate anyone that might have seen it. Aleksei will remove the computer disks and then you will pack it with C-4 and detonate it down to the bottom of the bay."

Dimitry had been glancing at Aleksei. *I can smell KGB all over that punk, he thought.*

"Why do I have to drag this little puke around?" Dimitry asked.

"Because he will be your spotter if you have to use this," the captain said, holding the AK-47 up. "And most important he will get those disks off of that thing. Dimitry, you don't know a floppy disk from a frisbee."

"Well, if he slows me down or gets in my way, I'll break his neck and send him down to the bottom of the bay, too."

"Dimitry, don't let your pride and anger jeopardize this mission," the captain said.

The group left the office and Dimitry and Aleksei returned to their bunks. The captain and the XO returned to the bridge. The XO asked, "How can you let that guy talk to you like that?"

Zharkov looked at the XO with that face that people fear and said, "Well, are you going to do it? Trust me, Dimitry is the only one on this sub that can pull this off, and not only that, but that satellite has a nuclear-powered generator."

Then the radio engineer timidly walked up to the captain again and handed him another note. The captain read it and ordered the helmsman to dive. It was nighttime but just before the sub went under, the captain took a quick look through the periscope. The captain

shook his head. Everything was green. He didn't know they had in-
stalled a night vision feature on the periscope; maybe the thing was
malfunctioning. The very last thing that he saw were three black dots
in the green light.

The periscope slipped under the ice.

CHAPTER 20

The droning of the AC-130's engines could be heard from the inside of the hanger. Karen had flown from Maui to Hickam Air Force Base in Honolulu and now walked up to a hanger, totally unsure about what was going to transpire. As she walked through a door into the hanger she was greeted by a Lieutenant Sorenson.

"Welcome, Dr. Harner," Lt. Sorenson said.

"Hello," she said with an uplift in her voice.

"Follow me, ma'am."

"Can you fill me in as to what's going on?"

"Your presence has been requested in Washington. Immediately."

"Well, I know that part."

"You will be filled in on the flight to California," Lt. Sorenson said.

He kept walking to the AC-130 and Karen was wondering what it would take to get a real answer. She was pretty sure she knew the reason for this trip. The lieutenant turned and handed her a pair of headphones. As they walked the noise increased to a deafening level. He stood to the side while she climbed the ladder into the fuselage of the aircraft. A staff sergeant pulled the stairs up, which closed the door. As Karen waited, she felt the lurching of the aircraft as it lumbered down the runway. As the staff sergeant turned and walked back through the aircraft, he summoned her with a quick wave, and she followed him towards the back of the plane. He pointed at the seat against the wall.

First class, she thought as she sat down. *These guys are as much fun as a sharp stick in the eye.*

She buckled the seatbelt and looked around the spartan cabin. There were many covered pallets down the center of the cabin.

I hope the guys that lashed this load down were in a better mood then the guys I just met, she thought.

The staff sergeant plugged something into the wall and reached over to her headphones and freed the cord from a rubber band. He unraveled the cord then plugged her cord into the wall.

"Can you hear me?" he replied.

"Yes," she replied.

He pointed to the front of the aircraft and said, "The bathrooms are right behind the cockpit, up front there. If you need to use the bathrooms you may walk around the aircraft, but you must keep your seatbelt on at all other times. We will be flying over water most of the way. There is a flotation device under your seat."

"How long is the flight?" she asked.

"Six hours. But we will be stopping in California, so three to California and then three more to D.C."

"What's on the menu?"

"I will bring you some MREs."

"Thanks," she barely mumbled.

"Any other questions, ma'am?"

"I was told I'd be briefed."

The staff sergeant said nothing. He just pointed at one of the tarp-covered containers in the middle of the plane. Standing beside the container was a tall man in a black suit and wearing sunglasses. He walked over to the woman and plopped down beside her. Before he slipped his sunglasses off, he glanced down at her breasts. Had at least one child, he thought.

Then the staff sergeant unplugged his headphones and mystery man plugged his in. She watched as the sergeant walked away.

"Hi, Karen," he said as he slipped his sunglasses off, revealing brown eyes and a practiced warm smile.

"Hello, whoever you are . . . and your name is?"

"That's not really important, now."

"Well, when will it be important? I'll be the one to determine what's important to me," Karen said, realizing that he was just trying to get a read on her. "I like knowing who I'm talking to."

"Well, I'm Jerry Jones."

"And what agency do you work for Mr. Jones."

"I work with the administration."

"Ahh, could you be a little more general."

The agent burst into a laugh, another practiced response. "You are feisty," he said.

"Are we going to keep playing this game?"

"What game is that?"

"Football, I guess, Mr. Jerry Jones."

He chuckled and realized this woman was not intimidated in any way.

"Why don't you think my name is Jerry Jones?"

"Because you have been lying since you sat down, and I'm just wondering if you are going to keep playing this game, because I can play, too."

"I work for the CIA, and my name is Warren."

"Okay, Warren, time to come clean if you want any cooperation from me."

He pulled an official ID out of his jacket and flashed it in front of her. She grabbed the ID and studied it.

"Karen, I am here as an official from the administration. There is a lot going on. Washington is freaking out and you are the expert on solar storms."

"Why the CIA, I thought they were a spy agency?"

"Good question."

"Well there is a lot worrying the administration and apparently the Russians are having trouble with one of their satellites."

"What kind of satellite?" Karen asked.

"Spy."

"Ah, all the pieces are beginning to come together."

"Yes, Dr. Harner, you suddenly have become very important to national security."

"And how can I help you?"

"My sources tell me that you have done a lot of research on electronics and solar storms," The CIA operative said.

"It was Karen's turn to laugh, "Sources?"

"Dr. Harner, I'm here to help you, and both of us could help our country," he said.

Karen let out a long sigh, "Okay, go for it."

"So my first question is, can this solar storm bring down an aircraft?"

"First of all, there are many types of solar storms. Many of them have no noticeable effect on our lives. However, the one we are observing now is the mother of all solar storms. It's called a CME or coronal mass ejection. It can throw solar gases and radiation out a million miles from the surface of the Sun."

"Okay, and my question about aircraft?"

"That is the least of your worries, unless you are in the aircraft. Anything with electronics can be affected."

"How about a satellite?"

"Again, anything with electronics," she said with a tone of indignation.

"So radiation! Are you saying someone is trying to nuke our birds?"

"No," Karen said, glaring at him. "Radiation does occur naturally in the environment, not just in the bombs that humans make."

"What else could be the effect of this C . . . whatever it was?"

"CME . . . well, we covered a lot of the bad parts of solar flares, planes coming down, satellites falling out of orbit, the power grid could have a massive failure and that could lead to even more problems."

The CIA agent just sat there, mouth agape. "I'll be right back."

He unbuckled his seatbelt, stood straight up and walked up to the cockpit and disappeared inside. About fifteen minutes later, the staff sergeant walked to the cockpit, stayed inside for a few minutes and then exited. The staff sergeant walked over to Karen with a packet of paperwork and sat down where the CIA agent had been.

"Ma'am," the balding staff sergeant began. "I need to brief you on flying in a supersonic aircraft."

"It's kind of late for that isn't it? We've been flying for almost an hour now."

"This plane is not supersonic."

"Okay, you lost me. Why do I need a briefing?"

"The decision has been made by the White House, that you will be flown from Miramar Marine Base to Washington, D.C. In an F-15."

She studied him for a few seconds and could sense the concern coming from him and everyone else on the aircraft. "Okay," she said.

For the next hour he went through everything from take off to pulling the ejection handles. Not recommended unless everything else went to hell in a hand basket.

When they landed at Miramar, she was taken into a briefing room and given more information. Then she was fitted into a G-suit to prevent loss of consciousness from high G forces. She was walked out to the runway and put into an F-15. Just one minute behind her a very good looking pilot climbed up to the cockpit and shook her hand. The noise from other aircraft around was too much to have a normal conversation. A technician helped her get strapped in and put her helmet on, while the pilot put his on and got seated.

The Plexiglass shield closed over both of them, reducing the noise considerably and, much like the AC-130, she was able to talk to the pilot in a normal voice.

"Good evening, ma'am."

"Hi, what's your name?"

"I am Lieutenant Colonel Mitch Thomas, and yours, ma'am?"

"First of all, don't call me ma'am. I'm not your mother and my name is Karen."

She couldn't see his face but she could tell he was laughing.

Why do these hot young studs always call me ma'am? I'm only thirty-nine and probably will be the rest of my life, she thought.

"Well, hi, Karen. I will get you to D.C. In one piece. Just a word of warning. The takeoff will feel very violent. Just tense your abdomen like they taught you in the briefing and you will be fine."

He wasn't kidding about the takeoff, but once airborne it was like they were floating on a raft in the ocean. Three hours later they landed in Washington, D.C., and walked into a hanger to be debriefed. As a limousine took her to the White House, the Sun was setting and she knew the fireworks were about to start.

CHAPTER 21

Shortly after Bjorn got the boys back, he gave each of them a sled dog of their own. Mostly it was to teach them to be responsible; Bjorn insisted that they take care of the dogs themselves. Romy received Wing Nut, and Remus got a dog named Sinker. Both of these dogs were wheel dogs, and they were harnessed right in front of the sled. A wheel dog had to be very powerful because sometimes the sled it had to be broken free from the ice. That was the wheel dog's job. Also, when they used a dog for skijoring, they would just use one dog, so the strong wheel dogs were often chosen.

The boys were ecstatic that they got their own dogs. But one day around the tent cabin they had quite a scare. Ursa had walked down into the dog yard and Bjorn thought it was lights out for the dogs; maybe the big bear had a bad day hunting. That's when the amazing part started. Ursa was playing with the dogs, as if he was a long lost brother. Bjorn thought it was like a cat playing with a mouse before it consumed its prey. But that wasn't the case here. Ursa and the dogs were wrestling and tackling each other but it was all in fun. And even though these dogs were bigger than the average sled dog, they would be no match for Ursa. But they showed no concern as they played like a group of adolescent boys.

Bjorn thought of a possible explanation for this behavior. Because Ursa was a male he was denied the enjoyment of raising a family. When males mated they left soon after and didn't stay around to raise the cubs. Little did Bjorn think that his life was following that same pattern. But now that he had the boys back, he was going to try to change that. And Ursa relied on the sled dogs and even Bjorn and the boys to fill that empty gap in his life. This was all happening with some extreme consternation on Bjorn's part because if the bear was having a bad day or if he was hungry the whole family could disappear in an instant. That's when Bjorn considered starting to feed the bear when he looked hungry. Then there was the incident with Romy riding the bear and Bjorn chastising him for that activity. Romy stopped riding the bear, at least when Bjorn was around.

But one day when Bjorn couldn't find Romy or Ursa, he summoned Remus and they followed the big bear tracks up into Harrison Canyon. Romy could communicate with Ursa better than anyone else. There was something about the clicks and sounds that Romy used that Ursa keyed into or understood. So Bjorn and Remus followed the tracks up to where the tusk protruded from the bank and that's where they found Romy and Ursa.

"Click, click, whir, Umpf, click, umpf, whir," Romy said as he pointed to the bank.

"I can't believe this shit, the bear looks to be following his directions!" Remus said.

"Well, let's see what they are going to do."

"Looks like Romy has a plan," Remus whispered.

The bear had a look of confusion on his face, and then he walked over and sniffed the tusk. Ursa looked at the boy and he pointed at the tusk.

"Whir, whir, click, umpf," Romy said as if he was cheering on a linebacker. The bear pawed at the frozen bank and despite the fact that the tusk was firmly attached to the same, Romy was convinced they could get it out.

The bear pawed at the frozen bank. Even with six inch long claws it was like he was scraping on solid rock. It was like he was scraping his claws on solid rock. Ursa looked at Romy and the boy just pointed at the prize. Ursa walked over to the tusk and then wrapped his enormous mouth around the dirty white tusk with his three inch canines digging in.

Bjorn thought he heard a growling sound as the bear started to lean into the task, like a dog playing with a toy. Unexpectedly the tusk shifted and Ursa leaned his massive bulk into the challenge. Although Bjorn was bewildered by the scene, he had long since stopped preventing Romy's interest in the bear.

Soon another four feet of the tusk emerged from the bank and Ursa dropped it in the river, sniffing his successful accomplishment.

"Whaaaaaa, whaaaa!" Romy was cheering the victory, and dancing around with his hands above his head. Only then did he see Bjorn and Remus watching the scene. All Bjorn could do was shake his head in disbelief. Hearing Romy cheering with joy took him back to the day of their birth, when both kids were announcing their entry into the world. His mood darkened for a moment, knowing that Sarah wasn't here with him and the boys to celebrate this momentous occasion.

Now what the hell are we going to do with that? Bjorn thought.

The next day Ursa was hunting out on the bay and was successful getting a ring seal. While Ursa was away, Romy was very sad. This was no different than a boy and his dog. Bjorn was hoping that Wing Nut would fill that part of Romy's life, but he still was despondent. The day Romy rode the bear was proof that the two had a blood bond, stronger than any he had seen before. Stronger even than Remus and Sinker. If Romy had been allowed to choose, he would even have snuggled close to Ursa to sleep on the brutally cold "three dog nights." However, Bjorn was uncomfortable with Romy spending too much time with the bear.

For Ursa, having the humans around was a strange experience and he did his best to respect the distance that was required, but Romy didn't follow that rule either. Most importantly, Ursa made it his responsibility to keep other curious bears away because this was now his family.

One night out on the bay with the sky a neon green color, Ursa was on a hot track for a good meal. He could smell the ring seal under the ice. Just before he was about to pounce, the ice about thirty feet away from him fractured with a deafening roar and for the first time in his life the undisputed king of the Arctic ran away in fear. The bear turned and looked back at the frightening noise and to his surprise a black tree seemed to be growing up out of the bay and that was soon followed by a black monstrosity that looked like a cliff growing in the bay. When things calmed down a little the bear settled down and lay down on the ice. His were the only eyes that gazed upon this eerie sight.

Within an hour the black cliff began to sink back down into the icy waters of the bay, until all that remained was the tree and that faded down into the icy water, too.

CHAPTER 22

He got the page at 3:30 in the morning, which was lousy, because he had just met the girl lying beside him. A few hours ago he walked into a bar where he had gone to shake some of his tensions off. He was minding his own business when this blonde vixen walked up to him and started making the move on him. Chris Boxwell was one of those guys etched out of stone like some Greek sculptor had just finished carving him. Tension was what he had for breakfast, lunch and dinner as a Delta Force operative. He came to the bar to chase the tensions away.

After the initial get to know you talk, which he carefully censored because of the nature of his work, he asked her if she would like to go for a walk. But she had other things on her mind, because they didn't get far when she grabbed him and planted a lip lock on him. He asked if she would like to go back to his place, which she acquiesced to, knowing full well what this was leading to.

It was the best sex he had ever had, because she was a responsive lover, she liked it rough and she was a beautiful woman with a personality that matched his style perfectly. Her temper was a little on the bellicose side, but that was exactly what he wanted in his women.

Without a good temper it was like screwing a dead fish, so this chick was right up his alley.

On the third go round, she asked to be tied to the bed, because she loved it when the man was in control. Chris thought about that for a few seconds, because if he wasn't careful it might look like it was forcible sex and that could end him up in a place he didn't want to be. But he was very good at tying people up so he followed her instructions and the sex went over the top with her screaming at the top of her lungs at the moment of orgasm.

Receiving the page, Chris Boxwell was now in a tight place, but he was a specialist in dealing with tight places. The girl was a little more than drunk and she had slept through the pager beeps. What was he going to do with her? The page was summoning him to the base because they had a mission.

But he couldn't leave her in his apartment, too many weapons and other sensitive material, and he didn't want to kick her out in the street either. So he decided to use the one thing that would accomplish his goals, her temper. He was also trying to keep her on his radar after this mission. That's when it came to him, an illness. So he stuck his finger down his throat as far as it could go. And even though his stomach was empty with the exception of a few beers, that beer along with bile and stomach acid made for quite the impression.

She was lying face down and he vomited on the bed just as she shifted her position. Chris proceeded to vomit not only on the bed, as she moved and rolled right into the pile and then the rest of the vomit landed on her abdomen.

So much for keeping her on his radar, he thought.

She woke up startled as the burn of the stomach acid and the odor brought her around.

"What the fuck are you doing?" she shouted.

"Ohhh," he moaned, trying to whine in a convincing way.

As she came around to full wakefulness she screamed.

"Did you just barf on me?'

"I am so sorry, I feel terrible, can you take me to the hospital?"

"Noooo, I can't believe you just did that."

"Well, can you just call me an ambulance?"

"Call it yourself, you idiot," she yelled as she stormed into the bathroom to take a shower, slamming the door as she went.

Yup, the radar is definitely off line, Chris thought.

When the shower ended he picked up the phone and dialed 911. As she walked out of the bathroom dodging another pile of vomit, the paramedics were at the door. She didn't want her face seen so she brushed by them and sauntered out the door and into night that had a slight green look to it, kind of like the puke she had just washed off her skin!

He was still whining in the background as she left. As she heard her walking down the stairs he did a complete reversal.

"I'm fine, guys, I don't need your help or a ride to the hospital," Chris said.

"But a minute ago you were moaning in pain," the lead medic said.

"No, I'm fine, my girlfriend called 911 even though I told her not to."

"Okay, sign this refusal and we will leave you alone."

He quickly scratched his signature on the form and the paramedics headed for the door as he walked over and glanced at the parking lot from his window. A cab was just leaving the parking lot, so he figured he was in the clear.

Successful mission. Oh well, I could have used a good relationship right about now, he thought.

He had been assigned to the Unit for five years and had been on several big missions, but mostly to jungles or deserts. The biggest dangers were heat stroke and heat exhaustion, so this would be a new experience.

He jumped into his Corvette and headed to Fort Bragg. When he arrived, Harlan Mckenzie, director of the CIA, and several generals for the special forces were there. They had already begun the briefing.

"Nice of you to join us, Commander Boxwell," Mckenzie said.

"Sorry, sir. My girlfriend had a medical emergency."

"Is she okay?" Mckenzie asked.

"Yes sir, just the stomach flu."

"Do you want to stand down on this operation?"

"No, sir, her parents are going to meet her at the hospital."

"Yeah, but are you going to be distracted?"

"No, sir, I've prepared for this eventuality."

Mckenzie made no response, just gazed at Chris in silence, trying unsuccessfully to read him.

"Okay, let's move on with this," one of the generals said.

"To catch the late arrival up on the details, a Russian spy satellite is in trouble and will probably come down in the Northwest Territories of Canada. We want to be the first to welcome it."

"That's a big area. Can you give us a tighter area to concentrate on?" one of the operatives said to generalized chuckles around the room.

"Yeah, smart ass, NORAD has given us a rough idea of where it is going to land. And you are going to do a High Altitude Low Opening insertion."

"Sir, if I may interrupt," Chris Boxwell said, "if we jump at thirty to forty thousand feet at night, we could be looking at forty to fifty degrees below zero and even lower with windchill."

"Damn, they don't make 'em like they used to," Mckenzie said with a sneer.

"We have to be able to use our fingers to be an effective fighting force."

"So what do you suggest, do you want me to have a hot tub waiting for you?"

This comment didn't produce a laugh because the operatives knew this CIA guy was trying to put them down, on a mission that would make him cry. They all secretly wanted to rip his throat out, and many of them imagined that.

"No, sir, but there aren't many mountains in the area, so we could do a Low Altitude Low Opening drop. It will still be cold, but we will be on the ground a lot quicker."

"Oh, you'll be on the ground a lot quicker, in what condition I'm not sure," Mckenzie smiled, trying to ease the disdain he was feeling from the entire room. Harlan Mckenzie hated these warrior types and had disliked these guys since his days in Vietnam. All kinds of one-upmanship were going on here. Harlan saw himself as more of a psychological warrior.

"Okay, if you guys want to do it that way, it's not my ass." Mckenzie said.

Several of the operatives threw glances around the room and then at each other. They knew they could do a low altitude insertion, and without question it would be safer at these temperatures.

"We know what we're doing," Boxwell said.

"You know then, that you will be jumping at two hundred meters, there will barely be enough time for the chute to open, and forget about the reserve chute."

"Yes, sir, we've practiced these jumps before. If your chute opens you are on the ground three or four seconds later, and we will be using static lines, so there is no delay in pulling the cord," Chris said.

All Mckenzie could do was shake his head as he looked around the room at the men.

"Okay, let's continue the briefing," the director said.

The briefing continued covering all things expected and unexpected. The plan was to fly out of Grand Forks Air Force base, where they would stage until they knew the final drop zone of the satellite. Then they would fly clandestinely into Canada. Grab as much of the satellite as they could safely recover and then return to Grand Forks, North Dakota.

"I tried to get the new Apache for this mission, but they haven't been released yet. Therefore, you will be using a pair of Bell 205s that are already in Grand Forks Air Force Base. They are a proven aircraft for this environment," Mckenzie said, as he looked at the air force colonel in the meeting, who was nodding.

"So we are using choppers, but you still want us to jump on this. Why don't we just set down nearby and walk to it?" Boxwell said.

"Simply because the Russian government and the KGB are very aware that this is going down."

The attention of everyone in the room immediately picked up.

That could change this mission completely, Boxwell thought.

"If you encounter anyone out there, we will want to talk to them back at Langley." The team snickered a bit, knowing that they were going to the middle of nowhere and it was still winter up there.

"Yeah, maybe we can all get a polar bear to bring home with us," one of the operatives said, to a chorus of laughter.

I hope these guys do run into a polar bear. Then they wouldn't be so cocky, Mckenzie thought snidely.

CHAPTER **23**

In 1989, the F-15E was a new design for the air force and had just been introduced. Therefore this was a test flight, but this was also a matter of national importance. It was unusual that a civilian would go for a ride in an air force aircraft, especially a new one. But when the commander in chief calls, the rules are sometimes overlooked, chiefly because Colonel Thomas was a skilled test pilot. Also, this was a case of national emergency and the woman in the back seat might be instrumental to solving this crisis. The takeoff was indeed gut wrenching.

I wonder if these throttle jockeys can take that time after time, Karen thought.

For some reason, though, the landing was even scarier, possibly because Colonel Thomas seemed tense. But after the jolting touchdown and the reversal of the engines which thrust them forward in their harnesses, they finally rolled to a stop.

"Welcome to Andrews Air Force Base, Dr. Harner," Colonel Thomas said.

On the flight over they had gotten on a first name basis and Mitch had dropped the ma'am title, but out of respect he addressed her with her official title. During the flight the eerie green of the sky was enough to make the toughest of pilots a little nervous. It looked like a huge Easter egg hovering above them which was very appropriate because that holiday was coming up. Since it was dark out, the green color made Karen a little more comfortable because she had studied the aurora borealis for many years and it took her back to a time in her teen years that was etched in her memory.

I hope that Bjorn didn't have too ugly a death, she thought. *It's a shame, he was such a good man.*

But Karen knew the potential of this green color, especially this far south. Once they were on the ground, Karen began to get more anxious, because she had her work cut out for her. When Mitch opened the cockpit cover and the long Plexiglas dome lifted, Karen felt a cold breeze even in her flight suit. A black limousine was waiting by the terminal. A Secret Service agent and Jay Riley walked out to the F-15 while they rolled a staircase next to the aircraft so the pilot and passenger could disembark. Karen's legs were a little wobbly due to being immobile for so long.

"Hello, Dr. Harner, how was your flight?" Jay asked.

"Incredible," she said as she spun around and waved to Colonel Thomas. "Colonel Thomas really knows his stuff."

"Well, I'm Jay Riley, science advisor for the administration."

"Hi, Dr. Riley, I've been looking forward to meeting you."

"You are here because I've heard that you really know a lot about solar storms and the damage they can do to the things that we feel are essential for modern life."

"Yes, but I don't have very good news for you and the administration."

"Is this time sensitive?"

"Twenty-four hours," Karen responded.

"Well, let's get you to the White House."

They merged onto I-495, which is the major interstate around the capital and it was surprisingly busy at two in the morning. Most of the traffic was due to people gawking at the amazing northern lights. Karen didn't care that much about the lights; they were the icing on the cake. Karen was much more interested in what caused "the pretty lights." It was very worrying that the sky was green this far south. She could only imagine what it looked like further north in the Canada and Alaska.

Karen was taken through a series of advanced inspection methods, including X-ray and a thorough pat down by a female Secret Service agent, and then into the White House. She was taken to an elevator with Jay Riley. The ride on the elevator seemed long, as if they were descending very deep into the ground. When the doors opened more Secret Service agents were waiting. They escorted the two down the hallway to the situation room.

This room was long and not too wide inside. There was a long table with at least thirty chairs around it. Five people, including the military brass, were seated around the table already. When the group entered, the people at the table stopped talking. They turned to the newcomers and stood to greet them.

"Welcome, Dr. Harner, the president and the rest of the administration will be joining us shortly," a three star general said.

Karen started to feel a little light-headed with the importance of the event. It was beginning to take on such a wave of importance.

Which it should, she thought, *considering all the research I've had done on this phenomenon, I'm the only one in this room that knows the danger.*

She was glad the administration was taking this seriously. Then her thoughts went to Luna; she didn't have time to see her daughter before she left. All she could do was scribble out a quick note. As she sat there waiting for the meeting to start, she wondered if and when she would see Luna again. Karen spent the rest of the time organizing her notes,

The next person to walk in the room was Harlan Mckenzie, and Karen had an instant feeling that they were connected, but not in a good way. She got a creepy feeling from this man, and she didn't know why.

CHAPTER 24

Sinker had been nervous all night but as daylight broke he began to settle down. The strange night sky, where night had become day, was upsetting to all the animals. Since dogs can sense an earthquake coming, Sinker and the other sled dogs were on edge with the constant light in the night sky. Bjorn and Remus wondered if the dogs could sense the geomagnetic fluctuations in the atmosphere or was it just the eerie lights. Remus walked around the dog yard feeding the dogs. The lights had faded with the Sun coming up.

Sinker sniffed the meal, and as he did Ursa walked up. The dog immediately bared his teeth to the bear to show him this was not a good time. Daylight had stretched into six hours now and Bjorn and Remus were able to get some good hunting in. They had been working hard to restock the meat locker, and so Sinker was going to be rewarded with a large piece of caribou meat today.

Romy had moved back to the village to be with his adopted mom, Aga. The day he left with Wing Nut, Ursa came to the tent cabin looking for him. He smelled the scent he was looking for and began to follow the trail that headed north. He found Romy in the village, but the villagers were afraid of Ursa and Aga told Romy to send the bear away. So with tears in his eyes Romy gave his final clicks to Ursa and the bear walked away. The villagers had been lighting cracker shells to scare the bear away or to warn him to respect the humans in the village, even though Ursa wasn't that big a danger to the village. But no one knew the bear like Romy.

Sinker sniffed the meal and then gulped it in one bite. The huge polar bear had a good relationship with the sled dogs and he respected the message that was being given even though he was very hungry, too. The bear walked away and looked back at the dog, as if to say, "What did I do?"

Ursa eventually made his way out to the frozen bay in search of a ring seal. The problem for Ursa was a bear his size needed a near constant intake of food. He walked back to where he had seen the black cliff two days before. The hole in the ice had frozen over and there were chunks of ice scattered around the hole. But the most exciting thing was a ring seal was using the fresh hole to get air. As he explored the regions of the newly frozen hole, Ursa came across a strange black cable rising up out of the ice and lying across the surface of ice. It had a different odor than any he had ever smelled. Then Ursa found the black cord again. He pressed his nose against it and got a static electricity shock. It wasn't fatal but it shocked the bear, and he jumped back like a startled puppy.

Then he snuck up on the cord again, and being a forgiving creature, he wanted to give the cord another chance. When his nose got close he was shocked again. What did the bear ever do to that cord? His patience had reached its end. The bear stood up on his hind legs and came down with a ton of force on the cable and one of his six inch long claws cut the cable against the ice.

The radio engineer in the Akula sub received another message from the KGB at the base. He immediately took it to the captain, who was in his quarters.

"Come in," the captain shouted.

The radio engineer timidly entered the cabin.

"A message from the base, sir."

"Well, read it."

The engineer's eyes dropped. He was hoping to escape the captain quickly. The captain saw this as a sign that he could abuse the frightened man.

"Akula 23, Cosmos 956 is losing altitude, unable to retain orbit, will come down near 90 degrees longitude by 55 degrees latitude, will probably come down between 0000 hours and 0800 hours tomorrow, if possible. . . ."

The captain glared at the man, while he waited for the rest of the message. "If possible, what?"

"I'm sorry, sir, I lost communications with the base at that point. I made many attempts to re-contact them without success."

"What, you idiot, that was the most important part of the message! Do you like the sound of a Siberian vacation? Get out of here!"

The blushing engineer scrambled to leave the cabin.

The captain cradled his cranium in his hands. *If possible, If possible. . . . What? Well, it's the KGB and they always expect the impossible. I have Dimitry to do my bidding. If I know the KGB they would want us to bring the entire satellite back to the homeland, but they will have to be satisfied with sending it to the bottom of the bay,* the captain thought.

CHAPTER 25

It was March 12 in the year 1989. The Secret Service agent opened the president's bedroom door and walked over to his bed. He heard the snoring from either the president or the first lady.

"Mr. President," the agent whispered. And then he placed his hand on the president's shoulder and increased his volume slightly.

"Mr. President."

"Whoa, what, huh?" The president mumbled as he came out of a deep sleep.

"Mr. President, we have a possible threat to the country developing." The agent was still trying to whisper. But the first lady was beginning to stir.

"Hey, who are you and what are you doing in my bedroom?"

"Sir, I'm with the Secret Service."

"Oh, okay, yeah, I remember now."

"Honey, what's going on?" the first lady said.

"Nothing," the president said, "try to go back to sleep."

As the president walked out into the hallway the Secret Service agent said, "Mr. President, there are several people down in the situation room who will brief you."

"Is the cabinet going to be there?"

"Yes, sir."

As the president walked through the doors of the protected conference room, he could see a group of familiar faces and some that weren't as recognizable. The clock on the wall said 3:00 a.m. The vice president was there as well as the chief of staff and the chief of the Central Intelligence Agency. Also the science advisor Jay Riley was sitting beside a woman whom he didn't recognize. And there were other members of the cabinet who he was a little vague on.

"Mr. President, I'll get to the pressing issue of this situation. This is Dr. Karen Harner. She is one of the best solar astrophysicists in our country," Riley said.

"Hello, Dr. Harner," the president said, thinking he had heard that name before, but he was in a little bit of a fog.

"Hello, sir," Karen said in a forthright manner. She hadn't gotten her legs under her yet, but she knew if she was going to make it in this arena, she could not be intimidated by any of these power players. She had moved to Hawaii and in doing so she had left the mainstream of American society. So this was a very foreign environment to her.

The President of the United States sat trying to think of what to say next.

"Mister President, Dr. Harner has been studying solar storms for many years and a disturbing event has occurred. That's why she was summoned here," Jay Riley said.

"I know, that's why I told you to get her here. Go ahead with your presentation, Dr. Harness."

"Ah, my name is Karen Harner, sir."

"Okay, tell me what I need to know."

"Yes, sir, well, to start with, the Sun has an eleven-year cycle. Every eleven years we reach the solar maximum. That's where we are now."

"Okay," the president said.

"I recently observed a very large solar storm. We call them coronal mass ejections or CMEs."

"And what's going to happen, except a big Easter egg in the sky? And it's a little early for Easter, got a couple weeks, I think."

"Well, sir, there could be a cascading series of problems with ever increasing intensity."

"So is the Sun going to explode or something?"

"Not really, but a large chunk of it has erupted out into space."

"How big a 'chunk' are we talking?" Jay Riley asked.

"Well, first of all, you need to understand that the Sun is not made of rocks; it is made primarily of hydrogen gas. So when I say a chunk, I am talking about a similar effect of popping a balloon with propane in it next to a candle. It will be a huge explosion, but the Sun is 93 million miles away from us."

"So how big an explosion are we talking about?"

"Through the telescope at the Mees Solar Observatory, I saw an explosion that I estimated at 10 million tons of plasma. You understand that this has already happened, we just haven't felt the effects of it yet."

"And what will be the result of that?"

"Well, solar plasma has a magnetic field to it and as it enters our atmosphere, it will cause electrical currents to spike throughout our power grid. That will fry a lot of transformers and the entire power grid will collapse in a wave."

The entire room drew a big but silent breath. Karen looked around the room.

Well, now I have their attention, she thought.

"There's no way our power grid could fail; it's been running for hundreds of years, and the Sun must have belched many times, in that stretch of time," the president said.

"Actually, the last known CME of this size happened, we think, in 1859. It was called the Carrington Event."

"And the planet is still here; we weren't knocked out of orbit or anything," the president said.

"Well, the difference is that now we live in a very electronic culture. In 1859 there weren't any power grids, and definitely no computers," she said.

"So we could be a lot more vulnerable," one of the generals said.

"Exactly, but I'm not finished yet. Once the power grid fails, nuclear power plants would go off line and the spent fuel rods would over heat and release their radiation. No power means that all the refrigerators in this country would fail unless people have generators, food would spoil and the food supply would be disrupted. I'm not sure what would happen but total anarchy could ensue."

"Well, aren't you the harbinger of bad news?" the vice president said.

"No, sir, I'm the harbinger of reality.'

"Anything else?" Jay Riley asked the question no one else had the courage to ask.

"Lots," Karen said.

"Well, we are the strongest country in the world, so we will prevail," one of the generals said.

"Yes, sir, but our country is only as strong as our aircraft and tanks. Anything with electronics could be taken out by this CME. You see this hasn't happened in the modern era, so we don't have a lot of information yet, and we can only estimate the level of damage."

"So what's next?" Riley asked.

"Well, aircraft would not be able to fly, and I think the biggest reason I was called here is that satellites would fail and drop out of orbit. GPS systems would also be ineffective."

"Is it possible this CME could have brought down this Russian satellite?"

"It depends on the amount of insulation it has to protect it from the power surges and radiation. So my answer to that question is, it is possible—absolutely."

"Well, how can we protect our equipment?" the chief of staff asked.

"You can't just wait until the CME is finished and hope things will return to normal. It depends on the intensity of the CME, and by all indications this looks like a large scale storm!"

"So what can we do?" Riley asked.

"If you see power grids starting to fail, shut them down, and hopefully nothing will get fried. If you shut down the power grids that will probably spare the transformers," Karen said.

"But people won't have power."

"You have to make the choice; it's like a game of Russian roulette, either shut down the power and people will be without it for a couple days or leave it up and when the power grid fails it may take months to restore it."

That left an ominous feeling in the room but everyone knew the right choice.

"Well, we will have to cancel Easter," the president said.

Karen's head snapped around to stare at the president. She was speechless.

"It's okay, Mr. President, we'll take care of everything," Vice President George Brown said.

"Good job, Brownie," the president said.

As the meeting broke up, the president said, "General, can you get a team of commandos going to the area where you think that trashed satellite will be coming down?"

"Yes, sir, Director Mckenzie has already briefed a team and they will be en route as soon as you push the button."

"Then let's push the button."

"Waiting for your command, sir."

"It's a go, deploy the team."

"Yes, sir."

CHAPTER 26

The captain of the Akula sub didn't want to show his position during daylight hours, but the clock was ticking now because the satellite was coming down. They barely broke through the ice with just the top of the conning tower in the frigid air. The periscope went up and the captain took a look around. They refreshed the air tanks and the captain spotted the communications cable. He could see the cable had been severed and he also saw huge tracks around the area.

What the fuck was that? he thought. *What is out there, some kind of a monster?*

He spun the periscope a full 360 degrees, slowly studying the ice. He saw a featureless expanse of ice in every direction. He saw nothing but a few ice ridges in the green light.

"Helmsman, reel in the communications cable and let me know when it's in," the captain said.

"Yes, sir."

"Then I want you to submerge and take us to a heading of eighty degrees longitude by fifty-five degrees latitude," the captain said.

"Aye, captain."

The sub dropped down to seventy-five feet and was under way. Once the helmsman was in control, the captain walked down to where the communications cable was stored. A couple of ensigns were holding the end of the cut cable. When the captain walked into the room, the conversation ceased and the men snapped to attention.

"At ease," the captain said. "Let me see that cable."

One of the ensigns picked it up and handed it to the captain. The captain examined the sliced cable.

"What could have done this?" he asked almost rhetorically.

One submariner glanced at the other to see who was going to speak first. "I don't know, sir."

"Well, if you had to guess, what would you say?"

"Something manmade like a knife."

"There were tracks around the cable this big," the captain said, holding his hands two feet apart. Then he looked at the submariners.

"Were they snowshoe tracks?" the other ensign replied.

"Well, this is a reasonably clean cut, but who the hell would be walking around out there, it's freezing."

"Maybe some one is stalking us," the first ensign said.

"Someone . . . or something?" he asked with a fearful but malicious look in his eyes.

The two ensigns looked at each other, unsure of what to say.

Word moved around the sub, and as it traveled from one person to the next it grew from a myth to a legend, growing larger and larger. Being locked in that steel tube for a long time can play tricks on one's mind. Very few of the submariners conversed with Dimitry, because his legend had reached a level that no one wanted to mess with him. But he overheard the story as it grew. His imagination ran wild, because he wanted to leave a legacy like the one that followed him from Afghanistan. Dimitry's heart started racing. He had a chance to fight a real demon. He paced back and forth in the sub waiting for the order to go. He was like a chained dog eyeing a rabbit, just out of reach and salivating over the taste of that tender meat that he couldn't quite have. And even better, if he faced a worthy adversary he would be a legend.

Aleksei, on the other hand, was preparing for a KGB mission and he was equipped for the possibility of a situation like this. In a cabinet under his bunk he had a PP90M1 submachine gun. He strapped on the custom-made harness that allowed him to carry the weapon under his clothes and he packed the magazine full of armor-piercing rounds that could penetrate ten millimeter steel plates.

In addition to that he carried five magnetic packs of C-4 for sinking the satellite if the opportunity came. Both of them prepared the necessary clothing for the brutal weather. It took no longer than one hour to reach eighty degrees longitude by fifty five degrees latitude. Since they didn't have communications with the base, and it was daylight out, the captain decided to wait until dark and than take a peek.

The Delta Force team had flown to Grand Forks Air Force Base during the night and then spent some time a preparing their equipment. There were a dozen members of the team—six commandos were on the assault team, two on the mini gun, one with an antitank rocket launcher. Then there was an explosives specialist, who had many different types of explosives, shaped charges and C-4. A communications specialist was also part of the team, and Chris Boxwell was in command of the team.

After they arrived at Grand Forks Air Force Base, they were tak-
en into a conference room. They were given snow cammo gear and
used white electrical tape to cloak their weapons. Then they did a
training session to get used to the frying pan–sized snowshoes.

Then they put together a practice mission to a frozen lake in
nearby Minnesota. Because this was a test to work out the bugs, it
was done during daylight hours. The Low Altitude Low Opening
was done at six hundred feet with static lines to deploy the chutes.
However, one of the parachutes was late in opening and stopped the
fall of the commando just twenty feet before he made a crater in the
ice. Therefore the jump altitude was changed to one thousand feet.
The entire team was given a quick briefing on the satellite and the location of the high valued parts. All the commands were carrying M1
submachine guns plus specialty weapons. Once night fell, the team
boarded the two Bell 205s and took off. They flew for two hours, and
as they approached the area one of the chopper pilots summoned
Boxwell to the front.

"Yeah, what's up?" Chris asked.

"We can see a dark, box-shaped object about a mile out on the
ice."

"Do you have an ID on the object?"

"Negative, and I'm not sure you want me to guess."

"Yeah, give me your best guess."

"It looks like a conning tower for a submarine, but I'm not saying
that positively."

"10-4," Boxwell said. Then he returned to the commandos.

"Penguin 2, do you have a copy? I want your three assaulters
to glide as far north as you can because we have a possible enemy

combatant unit north of us about a mile. Also take the rocket launcher with you."

"Copy that."

"If it turns out to be nothing then double-time it back to the primary location."

"Copy."

The helicopters flew in circles around the designated area, waiting for the goal to become visible.

The aurora borealis was flowing in loops and looked like thick green clouds, swirling in rolling waves. The commandos decided not to use night vision goggles because the northern lights were illuminating everything like the Sun. At 1800 hours the Akula sub surfaced, breaking the ice with a crashing sound that it always made during that operation.

Dimitry and Aleksei were on the ladder that ascends the conning tower. When the sub surfaced, the captain lifted the periscope to check out the surrounding area and hopefully spot their goal. Of course, all he saw was a green screen because of the aurora whirling and twisting from one horizon to the other. The sky was green, the snow was green and once he gave the order for Dimitry and Aleksei to disembark, they were green, too. In their cocoon known as a nuclear submarine, they couldn't hear the distinctive chopping noise of the helicopters circling.

No one saw the sub surface through the ice or the two helicopters circling, but three pairs of ears heard them. All hell was about to break loose.

CHAPTER 27

The flaming orb ripped through the veil of the aurora borealis like a ball parting a curtain. The lights visibly swirled as the wreckage cut through them. And as the fireball got closer it was followed by a flaming tail.

Bjorn and Remus were outside working on gutting their latest kill. It was possible to work as if it was daylight with the brightness of the northern lights. The first thing that told them something big was going down was the meat that they were working on brightened by many lumens, as if someone had just thrown a switch. They first saw the light on the meat, and then they saw their shadows extending out in front of them. When they turned their heads, they immediately jumped up to run.

"Oh shit, it's a comet," Bjorn said, as he ran with Remus close behind him. Then just as quickly as he began to run he stopped. The realization that they were most certainly going to die when this hit the earth sobered him up. Remus had almost caught up with him and was looking over his shoulder so he didn't see that his father had stopped.

The young man plowed into the older man as if he had tackled him. The two went down in the snow. Ursa was about a half a mile away, stimulated by the smell of fresh meat. The men usually left some meat for him. Little did he care that the parts that he got were parts the men couldn't stomach.

When the satellite suddenly showed itself, the big bear was startled. And just as any time a bear is frightened, he choose fight over flight. He rose up to his full ten foot height with his front legs stretched out in a menacing posture.

The sound of the falling satellite was a cross between a rocket engine and a sucking noise as the flaming wreckage cut through the air.

Chris Boxwell had just finished giving the new orders to Penguin 2 and was lowering his radio when the ball of flames appeared out in front of the chopper. The pilot of the Penguin 1 instinctively jerked the stick hard to the side, causing the chopper to dive hard. A variety of explicatives echoed around the cabin. Most of the commandos immediately thought, *Who is shooting missiles at us?* They braced for a very bad time about to happen.

When the pilot finally got the helicopter under control he was just over one thousand feet in altitude. Even though the commandos knew this event was going to transpire, it took them a second to realize they weren't under attack.

Unfortunately the commandos in Penguin 2 reacted a little too quickly. When they were shocked by the satellite someone yelled, "Abandon ship, deploy, deploy."

And without thinking about it, six commandos jumped out assuming they were under attack and would be better off taking their chances on their own. The problem was that they hadn't clipped their static lines into the ring at the top of the chopper. The commando with the mini gatling gun strapped to his back reacted too quickly and didn't clip into the ring and immediately went into the spread eagle skydiving position. Then he remembered and tried to fix the mistake by quickly pulling his ripcord. In spite of this, it was too late and with the extra weight, he hit the ice when his chute was still coming out of his pack. He died instantly.

The rest of the team on Penguin 2 was able to parachute safely down to the ice. Then they quickly went into operation mode. Even though they weren't expecting this twist, they trained for these surprises.

The commando with the communications pack took the lead for Penguin 2.

"Assault team, see if you can get on top of that conning tower," the leader said. The three assault team members started to make their way the one hundred yards to the sub.

"Rocket launcher, you stay with me."

"Yes, sir."

"Where is the mini gun?"

"Haven't seen him."

"Use your M1 and try to take out the lens on that periscope, and do it before the assault team gets there."

The commando with the rocket launcher lay down in the snow and set his sights on the top of the periscope.

The captain of the Akula sub was gazing through the periscope. He was getting bored with the featureless green view, so he deployed Dimitry and Aleksei. Then he thought the satellite had maybe come down miles away from here. He watched as the two men walked away from the sub.

He was gazing at the men when Aleksei began to run. Then the light was changing. It had a much more yellow hue. Aleksei was running in a panic but Dimitry was screaming at something unseen. As he watched a flaming object came into his view; it was turning over and over as it fell. He realized that this was the satellite coming down and hoped he hadn't deployed the men too soon.

CHAPTER 28

Karen had taken a break from the high stress of the situation room. At 6:00 p.m. On March 13 she was called back to the situation room. She had been accompanied by a female member of the Secret Service the entire time and was transported by a limousine back to the White House.

When she entered the situation room, the meeting was about to get started. The director of the CIA Harlan Mckenzie started the meeting by giving a briefing on the status of the troubled satellite. "About ten minutes ago NORAD reported the satellite had made impact somewhere up in Canada. They had been tracking it well before it passed Elmendorf Air Force Base."

"Where did it land?" President Hoaglund asked.

"It touched down just east of the of the west shore of Hudson Bay."

"Are the members of the Unit on it?" one of the generals asked.

"I'm going to give that question to General Dewit, from Fort Bragg," Mckenzie said.

General Dewit addressed the gathering.

"The team deployed to the location where the satellite came to a stop. Unfortunately it came to a stop on Hudson Bay," General Dewit said.

"Why is that bad, isn't it at the bottom of the bay?" the president asked.

"Not yet, sir, there is two feet of ice on Hudson Bay, and when the satellite came through the atmosphere, it caught on fire, because of reentry friction," Genral Dewit said.

"Oh," President Hoaglund responded.

"However, we don't know how large the wreckage is, but if it continues to burn it will eventually melt through the ice and sink to the bottom."

"Is the team going to be able to recover it?" President Hoaglund asked.

"There is one more thing," Director Mckenzie spoke up.

"Oh, there's always one more thing," the president said in exasperation.

"Yes, sir," Mckenzie replied.

"What is it, director?"

"There are enemy combatants in the area."

"What did you . . . how did they get there?" President Hoaglund stumbled through his question.

"Sir, we have seen a submarine in the area. And we know it's not one of ours."

"Oh, shit, is the Delta Force kicking ass?" the president asked.

General Dewit interjected, "Sir, the team is still engaged in this operation. We will know pretty soon."

"General Dewit, I want your team to bring back anyone involved or witnessing this event to Langley for interrogation," Director Mckenzie said.

Karen was very intimidated by this meeting and this group and especially Director Mckenzie, but she braced herself and spoke up. "Mr. President, I would like to interview these people, too."

"Dr. Harner, forgive me, but this is a case of national security," the CIA director said.

"You're damn right it is, but if you think your biggest problem is one submarine, you, sir, are going to be in for a shock," Karen said.

The director stopped and turned to look at her as if to say, "Who do you think you are?"

"In what way, ma'am?" the vice president asked.

Oh, shit, here we go with the ma'am title again, she thought.

"If the power grid in this country fails, your problems will be off the chart."

"Yes, but that has never happened."

"But I think this CME will be bigger than any in modern times, and I need to talk to the people who witnessed the aurora borealis firsthand to get a handle on the size of this solar storm."

"Dr. Harner, does size really matter?" Mckenzie said, grinning.

"Yes, it does when you are talking about solar storms," she said. *And some other things*, she thought. But she knew he was just trying to break her focus.

"Sir, you can't let a civilian run the decisions of this administration."

"Mr. President," Jay Riley came to her defense, "Dr. Harner is the best expert this country has to offer in this field, she's been studying solar storms for ten years."

"Okay you can interview anyone you want to interview," President Hoaglund said.

Director Mckenzie frowned and glared at Karen but nodded his approval.

CHAPTER 29

Most of this planet is wet. Three quarters of the planet is covered by water. A lot of the land surface doesn't have people on it because it is inhabitable. Space junk falling out of orbit is rarely seen by human eyes because the chance it will fall in an area with people is low. So the fact that at least sixteen people witnessed the demise of Cosmos 956 was incredible.

Bjorn and Remus had a front row seat, and once they accepted that this would be their last day on planet Earth, they stood and watched the spectacle. The satellite was as big as a small school bus, occasionally turning over while falling and completely involved in flame, with a flaming tail that stretched out at least a mile behind it.

As Penguin 1 with Chris Boxwell onboard saw that huge flame thrower approaching, they decided to hold their deployment until the danger passed and they knew where it was going to come to a stop. Luckily for them the falling debris fell at least eight hundred feet below them. With their static lines clipped into the ring in the chopper, as many as could fit sat on the floor at the open door and watched the amazing sight.

While this was occurring, Chris called the commando who was running the other half of the operation and had the radio.

"Penguin 2, do you copy?"

"Copy, Penguin 1."

"All accounted for?"

"One unaccounted for, Penguin 1."

"Who's missing?"

"Haven't seen the mini gun yet. You going to join the fun down here?"

"As soon as we know where we're going."

"Copy that."

Dimitry was overjoyed by the turn of events, even though he knew a satellite was coming down. But he didn't realize he was going to face a fire breathing dragon. Aleksei had a hard time staying with the maniac running at full speed towards a certain death.

The two men had gotten far enough away from the sub that they didn't hear or see the Delta Force commandos silently gliding down. And the two men were wearing winter cammo also, so they were invisible as well. If Dimitry would have known he missed a good fight, he would have been very angry.

The satellite was falling west to east and looked like the setting Sun. It was coming down to earth at a thirty degree angle and got louder as it got closer to the ground. Bjorn and Remus were the only two involved who knew nothing of the satellite. They also knew nothing of the men who had joined them from distant places. Because of the noise from the satellite, they didn't hear the rotors of the helicopter. They were about a mile from the glide path of the falling satellite.

Sinker was howling his disapproval, and Ursa was mesmerized by the glowing light in the night sky.

The huge flaming mass hurtled closer to the ground, and when it hit, there was no huge explosion, no death. Just a very loud metallic crash, like a very big automobile accident. And the crash continued because the wreckage bounced, spewing parts and flames in every direction. Then the satellite bounced again, each time the bounces getting smaller until a flaming ball was sliding on the ice, and hissing like a hot rock being dropped in water. Steam rose as the ice was turned to water and water was turned to steam.

Bjorn and Remus just stood there in shock, staring at the incredible event. They still didn't know what had happened, and Bjorn immediately thought that it could have been an aircraft.

"Remus, let's get the dogs."

"Why?"

"That wasn't a comet. It could have been a plane."

"What's a plane?"

"You know those things that I've shown you up in the sky."

"Yeah, but they never come down to the ground."

That's when Bjorn realized that Remus had never been exposed to a world other than the one they lived now. Bjorn and Remus ran the short distance to get Sinker and another sled dog. In seconds they were on their skis and being towed by the dogs out to the wreckage. Because they were on skis and had dog power, they got to the satellite first.

At the same time Dimitry and Aleksei were were snowshoeing their way to the same place. Dimitry had a sniper rifle so he didn't need to get very close. After jogging half the way with snowshoes on he was breathing and sweating hard and Aleksei thought that he would freeze to death if he didn't meet his fate sooner than that. It took Aleksei five minutes to catch Dimitry and by that time he was in a prone position trying to sight in his sniper scope.

The three separate parties still didn't know about each other.

When the satellite came to a bouncing halt, the pilot put the chopper right above it. Then Boxwell said, "Go, go, go." The team had left the helicopter virtually at the same time and moved apart quickly so their chutes wouldn't tangle. They just barely separated enough because they were all on static lines.

If the wrecked satellite was the center of the clock, Bjorn and Remus and their dogs were at nine o'clock. Dimitry and Aleksei were at two o'clock and they were both prone and checking out the satellite and the surrounding vicinity. Then Penguin 1 started to glide silently in, and suddenly every one of the players was in the equation.

Meanwhile, the Penguin 2 commando carrying the rocket launcher was pulling off rounds at the top of the periscope. The Soviet captain was watching everything unfold from inside the sub, when suddenly his view fragmented and then turned black. He stood there for a second and then realized they were under attack.

"Submerge, submerge right now!" the captain shouted.

The helmsmen looked at him.

"Submerge, damn it."

"But we have two men on the ice!"

"Submerge!"

The helmsman quickly relayed the orders and started throwing switches.

None of the men knew about the one entity that would swing the balance of power completely.

CHAPTER 30

Jay Riley was nervous; his consternation was because the solar maximum would occur soon. It would all come to a head tonight. He wanted to stand behind Karen Harner and he knew she was right. But he worked for the administration and despite President Hoaglund's memory problems, he felt that standing with him would serve him best.

The power outages started in Ontario, which was closest to the biggest hit from the solar output. The outages continued rolling from power plant to power generators and taking out transformers as the surge overwhelmed the grid, one part at a time. The power surges that the CME started could not be stopped, but the damage could be reduced by shutting the power grid down.

The Canadian government was on alert when the choppers entered Canadian air space. The Hoaglund administration decided to do this in secret because they wanted the rewards of the satellite. They had scrambled F-15s but the helicopters flew under the radar. Then the power went down, starting in northern Ontario and continuing south until the outage took out Ottawa. Suddenly Canada declared a state of emergency and cancelled the search for the helicopters.

The outage was ruthless; it spared no transformers or power plants or even a lightbulb. It rolled into the United States at Massena, New York. The entire town of Massena went down in less than ten minutes, and then it continued south and west.

The Canadian government contacted the administration in Washington. Then the mayor of Massena called the governor of New York, who called the president. Suddenly the president's phone was ringing off the hook.

"Get that scientist back in here, now!"

"You mean Mr. Riley?"

"No, uh . . . uh, you know."

"You mean Dr. Harner."

"Yes, yes."

Karen was whisked into the situation room, where the group was in a turmoil. When the vice president saw Karen enter, he shouted, "Dr. Harner," and signaled her over. "We are having a lot of power outages."

She bit her lip to keep from saying "I know, what did I tell you?"

"What do we do now?" President Hoaglund asked.

"There is nothing you can do to get those damaged transformers back, however, you may be able to prevent more damaged equipment by shutting the power grid down."

"But that would deny most of our citizens power. We have discussed that and decided that we should not shut the power down and maybe the Sun will stop cooking our power system."

"Can this solar storm be harmful to humans?" the vice president asked.

"If you are asking can the radiation harm people, most likely not, but without power, there will be no traffic lights, leading to car accidents, and people will fall down stairs because the lights will be out, so indirectly, yes."

"Is there any other way to deal with this without shutting down the grid?"

"Actually, sir, there is something that I didn't mention."

"Go on," the vice president responded.

"We haven't tested this . . . however, the CME causes power surges, so when we shut down the grid, the power surges will about equal a normal level of power generation, so it's possible that people won't be inconvenienced that much."

They sat there stunned and they all looked at Jay Riley.

"Yes, I have heard rumors that were similar to this."

"We can't bet everything on rumors," the president said.

"Dr. Harner, will you give us some time to discuss this," the president said.

"You know this will not be like a hurricane, or tornado, or earthquake. They only affect certain areas at one time, but the grid going down could sweep across the entire nation. Those other disasters would be chump change, compared to this," Karen Harner said

She sat down and crossed her arms.

Soon the group of politicians with the president in charge decided to take a wait and see position.

She rolled her eyes and stormed out of the room.

"Take me back to my hotel," she said to the Secret Service agent.

CHAPTER 31

The rifle scope was fogging up due to the cold and Dimitry's hyperventilating. He had to remove his gloves and put his hands over the scope's lens to defrost it. Both Aleksei and Dimitry heard gunshots coming from the direction of the sub they had just left, but they were men on a mission.

However, these soldiers were used to gunfire after their time in Afghanistan and other conflicts. That's when Dimitry's eye peering through the scope started seeing the shadowy forms of the commandos. He also saw two other figures that weren't concealed with the white cammo, and it looked like they had two dogs with them.

Since his scope was still a little on the foggy side he moved the crosshairs over to one of the darker and more visible figures standing by the still burning satellite. That position illuminated the two men, which Bjorn would never have allowed if he knew there was a sniper rifle in the area.

The commandos were gliding silently down behind Bjorn and Remus, and even though Bjorn couldn't see them he sensed danger and was trying to figure out why the alarms were going off inside his brain. He assumed it was because he was standing beside an unknown wreckage, but he still felt an uncomfortable sensation, as if he was missing something.

Dimitry thought the two figures with the dogs were somehow associated with the commandos and people trying to steal Soviet secrets. He knew he had to eliminate these people.

Bjorn and Remus usually ran their dogs in single file to prevent dog fights, but when they came to the satellite they stopped side by side. Dimitry put the crosshairs on the right-side figure, clicked the safety off with his thumb and then slid his index finger over the trigger. Once he figured out the rhythm of his breathing and the crosshairs consistently settled in the same location after every breath, he was ready.

Just then the dogs, who had been sending signals to each other, erupted in a snarling rage. Dimitry pulled the trigger, but Remus had braced himself for the dogfight and instead of the round hitting him in the head, it grazed the top of his shoulder.

"Heeey, hey," the Bjorn and Remus yelled. And they started pounding on the dogs to break up the dogfight. Bjorn and Remus didn't hear the gunshot and Remus didn't really feel any pain. The dogfight was so distracting that when Remus started to try to separate the dogs, he suddenly realized that his left arm wasn't working. That's when a sharp burning pain started tearing through his whole left side. The bullet had fractured his left clavicle as it sliced through the top of his left shoulder.

"Dad, something is wrong with my arm," Remus said.

"What's wrong with it?"

"I don't know, it's killing me and I can't move it very well."

"Here, give me Sinker," Bjorn said.

Bjorn held the dogs apart on very short lines in an attempt to control them. He had no luck with that and the dogs started growling again. So he released them and they ran away to work out their differences on their own. Bjorn knelt down to help Remus and saw the torn parka and the blood flowing out.

Oh shit, what the hell kind of black cloud am I under? First Sarah died in a pool of blood, now Remus? he agonized.

"Don't you die on me," Bjorn said.

"I'm not dead."

"Yeah, but why are you bleeding?"

That's when the memories flooded back to him. He pulled Remus's parka back and saw the gunshot wound. Because of the distraction of the dogfight he didn't even hear the sound of the sniper rifle.

How did he get shot? Bjorn wondered.

"I'm fine, my arm is just aching a little."

"Son, you have a gunshot wound to your shoulder, and you are bleeding pretty badly."

Dimitry and Aleksei were lying prone at least two hundred yards away. They were separated by four yards. Ursa had shadowed Bjorn and Remus as they skijored down to the satellite. However, Ursa was very cautious around fire, so he started a circuitous route around the burning wreck. Then he smelled something else, other humans. So he went off to investigate. He came up behind Dimitry and Aleksei and that's when one of the men he was behind made a loud sound, a staccato explosion. And then he heard Sinker and the other dog sending signals as if something was wrong.

Then Remus fell and he knew something wasn't right and he decided to take action. He had to stop this. He walked up behind the men, and as Dimitry was preparing to take a shot at Bjorn, the massive bear rose up on his hind legs, just as if he was hunting ring seals and was trying to break through the ice. A ton of polar bear came down on the sniper and his two front paws landed on Dimitry's back just below his neck. The pile driver force crushed and fractured everything it landed on. Dimitry died instantly, as his vertebrae were pulverized and his spinal cord was completely severed in several places. The only noise was the impact of the huge bear, the cracking of multiple bones and a squeak as air was expelled from his lungs. He was dead.

Chris Boxwell heard the gunshot and saw the flash of the sniper rifle. Even though there were several distractions, including the burning satellite, the dogfight and the two Neanderthals, he managed to keep his focus and they immediately took up defensive positions until they could figure out who were friendlies and who were enemies.

"Penguin 2, we have a shooter."

"Penguin 1 assault team, he is directly on the other side of the satellite from our position."

The three assault team members started out separated into three different tracks and each one of them followed a zigzag course to the north. Boxwell and the two other members of Penguin 1, one with the sniper rifle and another who was trained in multiple skills, including paramedicine and as a spotter for the sniper.

"Penguin 2 assault team, cease and desist on the sub, we are headed south. Rocket launcher put a hole in that conning tower, once the assault team is clear."

"On the way, sir," the comm officer said.

Bjorn heard gunshots coming from the other side of the burning satellite and he immediately went into survival mode. Gunshots, circling choppers and now an explosion about a mile away, suddenly Bjorn was back in Vietnam. His training flooded back into his mind but he didn't have a gun to return fire. Remus was down holding his shoulder and Bjorn quickly dragged him behind the satellite.

Then he went into offensive mode. He still hadn't noticed the Delta Force team in a defensive stance in the background. Bjorn notched an arrow in his longbow and sent an arrow forty-five yards. It was a little long. Aleksei was lying prone but Dimitry had been annihilated by a creature that was bigger than any Aleksei had ever seen. Dimitry came looking for an adequate challenge and the challenge found him. Aleksei's heart was drumming frantically in his chest, and that's when something nailed his right calf down to the ice. He let out a long agonizing scream, which was part fear and part pain. Then Bjorn rolled over to face the sounds of gunshots and was facing six commandos, who were returning fire at whoever had fired that first shot. Bjorn had his large knife in his hand and was in a stance to take on whatever was threatening him and his son.

"Stand down soldier," Chris Boxwell said. He had recognized some military experience, and that's when he decided to address him as 'soldier.'

Bjorn instantly recognized that he was outnumbered by six commandos with firearms and immediately dropped the knife and raised his arms.

When the assault team rejoined the group of Penguin 2, they began to head south to meet the commandos from Penguin 1. They spread out so they couldn't be taken by a single missile or grenade. The comm officer stayed back with the rocket launcher. He gave the order to fire a rocket into the side of the conning tower and the commando with the rocket launcher complied as the sub was almost underwater.

The explosion punched a hole in the outer hull and cracked the inner hull. Then they caught up with the rest of the team. Within forty-five paces one of the commandos radioed the comm officer.

"Just found the mini gun," the commando said.

"What's his condition?" the comm officer replied

Thirty seconds went by. "KIA," the commando said and that news put an air of remorse over the Unit. But every team member knew every mission might be their last, and it just made them grit their teeth. They knew that their lives were less important than the mission and they accepted that. The men swore to themselves that they would not let his death be in vain.

"Mark the body with a timed strobe set for an hour and grab the mini gun," Chris Boxwell interjected.

"Already done," the commando said.

After Ursa killed Dimitry, Aleksei had rolled over and released a burst of lead from his M1 submachine gun. Two rounds flew safely by the bear, but the next one found a target. It lodged in his front leg. And even though the bear was wounded he grabbed Aleksei in his mouth and shook him like a rag doll. That started the screaming and then the arrow pinned him to the ice. Bjorn had fired an arrow blindly towards the direction of the sniper rifle's muzzle flash.

Since Ursa was wounded and the man wasn't moving, he limped away from the unmoving Russian KGB agent to lick his wounds. Penguin 2 stumbled on the two Russian soldiers. Aleksei was moaning in pain.

"Penguin 1, this is Penguin 2."

"Go ahead, Penguin 2," Chris said.

"Got two enemy combatants."

"Status?"

"Sniper is dead, spotter is wounded."

"Wounded by who?" Chris asked having not heard any additional gunshots. "Who was the sniper killed by?"

"Unknown, but it's pretty gruesome. The sniper has been implanted into the ice by at least a foot."

"Okay, mark the body with a timed strobe and bring the spotter here."

"Affirmative."

They quickly searched Aleksei and found the C-4.

The commando doing the searching jumped back with his gun drawn and shot Aleksei in his good forearm, so he couldn't trigger a switch to detonate the explosives. The rest of the commandos dropped down into defensive positions, ready to shoot at the least provocation.

"What the fuck are you doing?" the comm officer asked.

"This guy is wired, suicide bomber!"

"Why didn't you kill him?"

"Valuable source of info."

"No worries. Cuff him and let's start to carry him to Penguin 1.

"How did your friend get killed?" the comm officer asked.

Aleksei just stared into space. Then he half mumbled, half whispered, "Monster."

"He's worthless," the commando said

The commandos stripped him of all weapons and explosives and carried him to an area near the satellite.

Bjorn was trying to stop Remus's bleeding when all of a sudden he heard the cocking of a weapon behind him. He knew instantly what was going on and was taken back to Vietnam.

"You are the bastards that shot my son!" Bjorn said.

"No, the man that shot your son is dead." Chris said.

The special forces training started coming out of Bjorn. As he stood up and turned around to stare down the barrel of a submachine gun, he knew he was outgunned and outnumbered, so he quelled the urge to kill someone.

"Let my medic help your son," Chris said.

"He's bleeding pretty badly, so you will have to hurry."

"First, you need to lie face down on the ground."

Bjorn did as instructed and a commando put a zip tie around his wrists and patted him down. Then another one did the same to Remus. The commandos were amazed by the number of primitive weapons the two were carrying. By that time the entire Delta Force team was reunited. Chris and the comm commando had a brief conversation.

"Was that a Russian sub?" Boxwell said.

"Definitely," the commando said.

"Did you disable it?"

"Unknown, the conning tower took a hit from one of our rocket launchers, but they have a door which seals the conning tower off from the rest of the sub, so I can't say that it was disabled."

"Yeah, but if the conning tower fills with water the sub will float upside down."

"That will ruin their day," the comm's officer said.

"What are your thoughts on this piece of junk?" the commando asked.

"It's too big to haul in a harness under one of those choppers," Chris said

"It's too hot to take apart."

"So we could send it to the bottom and let the Canadian government deal with it."

"We can use the C-4 we pulled off the spotter."

"No, wait a minute, we have to try and get the CPU out of it."

"In about an hour we won't have a choice," the comm officer said, pointing at the growing pond around the hot satellite.

"Yeah, call in those birds; they probably have the tools we need to dissect this satellite. The comm officer called the helicopters, and they returned in five minutes. The commandos got the tools they needed off the helicopters. Three commandos climbed in one helicopter and returned to recover the dead commando and Dimitry.

Meanwhile, the medic, the comm officer and two other commandos moved Aleksei, Bjorn and Remus into the other chopper. That chopper became the medivac unit.

The Bell 205s were used in Vietnam and the sound of those choppers took Bjorn back to his days in Vietnam. All of a sudden he thought he was dreaming, surrounded by commandos and two choppers landing. *This is unbelievable. This can't be happening,* Bjorn thought. He had gone as far as he could to escape the war and the cruelty of the American society.

This was an apocalyptic scene right out of every nightmare he ever had. The CIA had tracked him down deep in the Northwest Territories. He had a deeper respect for that agency. Twenty years and thousands of miles away, they definitely had a long memory. He studied every face in the group of commandos to see if he recognized anyone.

CHAPTER **32**

The chief of staff for President Hoaglund's administration took the president into a private session away from all the cabinet members.

"Mr. President, if we shut down the power grid and it angers a lot of voters out there, it won't look good for your reelection," the chief of staff said.

"But what if the solar storm brings the grid down?" President Hoaglund asked.

"Then we can say it was an act of God," the chief of staff said.

"But the scientist says it could be worse."

"Yes, but no one has ever seen this happen and if she is right, we could look like heroes."

"Oh, I understand. And we aren't even sure if the whole nation is going to be affected."

"Correct, and this is March; the media and the public have very long memories, so if we shut the grid down, come November our names won't be worth a postage stamp."

"Right," the president said, with a confused look on his face.

"Now let's keep this to ourselves, the fewer people that know about this the better."

Director Mckenzie was very busy with this solar storm and the Russian satellite and getting the Delta Force team going. When he returned to his office in Langley, he was too busy to deal with the pile of memos. He even ignored the one on top of the pile. It was from the head of maintenance, telling him about the emergency generator, which was twenty years old and was showing signs of a looming malfunction.

The head of maintenance was requisitioning a new emergency generator, but he got no response from the director of the Central Intelligence Agency. Harlan Mckenzie was worn out after twenty-two years of espionage work. And something as minor as an emergency generator could wait until the next director took the reins. The rolling blackout continued rolling. At 1:00 a.m. it had made it halfway down the state of New York and the officials from New York were starting to panic. So far three people had died due to automobile accidents because the outage took out the traffic lights.

Before Director Mckenzie went back to the situation room in the White House, he stopped by Karen's hotel room.

"You can take a break," he said to the Secret Service agent. She walked away to get a cup of coffee, and Director Mackenzie knocked on Karen's door.

It took her a while to respond but eventually she opened the door slightly with the chain on it. She was blinking because she had been awakened from a deep sleep.

"Hello, Dr. Harner," the director said.

"It's one in the morning."

"We are being requested back in the situation room."

"I have nothing more to say."

"An idea has been proposed so we won't have to shut the grid down."

"What are you going to do, buy everyone in America a portable generator and put a cop at every traffic light?" Karen asked.

"Dr. Harner, you don't have to be so sarcastic."

"Well, get ready for a return to the 1800s."

"If that's what is going to happen, we will deal with it."

"Let me ask you, what's wrong with the president?"

"What do you mean?'

"He seems a little disconnected from reality."

"Well, why don't you get ready, and I'll tell you everything on the way to the White House."

Karen emerged from the room and the director nodded to the Secret Service agent and said, "I have a car waiting."

"Yes, sir."

As they walked down the hallway, Karen glanced back at the agent and said, "Don't we need the Secret Service agent?"

"Don't worry, Dr. Harner, I've been an operative for over twenty years."

"Twenty years?"

"Yes, ma'am."

"So you were in Vietnam?"

"Yup, I was the station chief of the CIA in Vietnam"

"Really?"

"Yes, I was," he said.

When they got out to the parking lot, the director stopped and turned.

"Dr. Harner, this administration is doing everything it can to prevent a calamity."

"Well, I'm sorry, director, but I would disagree with that."

"In what way would you disagree?"

"I've told the administration that if they don't shut down the power grid a rolling blackout will decimate this country."

"Well, ma'am, you don't know the drive that exists in this country."

"Are you insane, you mean to tell me that you are putting all the responsibility for an impending disaster on the people who will be most affected? If you plunge this country into darkness, you will quickly realize that willpower alone probably won't get us through this."

"Ma'am, I think you are overexaggerating this."

"Don't call me ma'am, you aren't that much older than me."

"Look, Karen, you are going to have the opportunity to interview the people who witnessed the failing satellite."

"That will be the best choice you've made since I've been here."

"Well, if the president didn't order it, I might not have allowed it."

"Are we done here?"

"No, tell me some other options to get out of this mess, other than shutting the grid down."

"Let me tell you something, take the damage from a 9.0 earthquake, a category 5 hurricane and an F5 tornado multiplied by one hundred and you may be getting close to the effects of this CME."

"You know, Dr. Harner, we understand you are just trying to help this country out, but you are a little misguided."

"I'm misguided!? You have some kind of agenda, which is controlling your choices," she said, realizing that her volume and tone had increased significantly.

"You don't want to shut down the power grid. Just follow the lead that the administration gives you and don't make any waves."

"And what if I follow my research and my sense of right and wrong?"

"You don't want to do this. . . ." He paused for a moment. "Don't forget about Luna."

She just stood there shocked, with her jaw hanging open, unsure of what to say.

"What? What did you just say?"

"You heard me."

"How did you know about Luna?"

"Karen, I work for the most advanced spy agency on this planet."

She suddenly remembered the CIA agent that met her in Hawaii.

"Don't bring Luna into this, she is completely innocent."

"That's good, let's keep it that way. Now let's get back to the situation room."

Karen realized that these people threatened others for a living and playing mind games was part of their technique. She stared at him, speechless, and tried to keep as much distance away from him as she could.

Was that a threat against her child? she wondered.

CHAPTER 33

The choppers landed, and the commandos got all the dead and wounded into one chopper, with the medic and a few other members of the team. The comm officer went with that trip, too. Even though Remus and Bjorn were innocents, no one knew that, and their hands were still bound behind their backs. Aleksei's hands were bound also and that brought loud objections from the KGB agent.

Bjorn was transported back twenty years to a time when he did this type of work. He was sitting quietly in the Bell 205, a chopper that he was very familiar with; in fact, he had been trained to fly one of these helicopters. He looked like a backwoods hillbilly but in his mind were years of special forces training and CIA tricks. He was dressed in furs but his mind was spinning like a top, with plans to free himself and his son because he had no idea what was happening.

On one of the choppers were an axe and a shovel. Lieutenant Boxwell sent the chopper that had become the morgue and medivac unit on its way back to Grand Forks. Then the other commandos began to work on getting the CPU out of the satellite. One of the members of the team started shoveling snow on the steaming satellite to cool it down. Once the heat had been brought back into reasonable range, they took the axe out of the chopper.

Some other commandos traced the trail back to the shore that the satellite had left on its bouncing demise. They were checking to see if any important parts had come off the satellite. While they were doing that, the rest of the team were using the axe to hack away at the guts of the charred, smoldering piece of junk. Unfortunately the axe was no match for the metal frame of the wreckage. The axe blade quickly accumulated large nicks and became very dull.

The explosives expert just stood there shaking his head. He walked through the icy water to the satellite, looked at the commando hacking away and yelled, "Hey!" The other commando stopped his work and looked at the explosives expert.

"What?"

"Is there going to be anything left of that?"

"Do you have a better idea?"

"Lieutenant Boxwell," he shouted.

Chris waded out to the satellite and asked, "You have a plan?"

"Yes, sir, I have some small shaped charges and if I put one here, here, here and here we can cut the CPU out of the heart of this satellite ," he said, pointing to the locations.

"You're not going to send it to the bottom, are you?"

"No, sir, I can shape some C-4 so it will be a very controlled blast. Then we'll be able to pick the brains out of the satellite and carry it to the chopper."

"Well, what are you waiting for, let's get it done."

The explosives expert climbed up on the twisted steel and carefully placed his charges, then inserted blasting caps in each and set the timers for 3:11 a.m. Then he casually walked behind the ice fracture to where the rest of the team was waiting, and exactly one minute later, six simultaneous explosions produced a rather muted bang. Then they walked back out and all but one support was completely severed.

He picked up the dull axe and with one swing the CPU of the satellite dropped down into the frozen water. He signaled to another commando and they lifted the processing unit up to carry it away from the wreck. The two commandos could see through the water and ice because the heat from the satellite had melted the snow and much of the ice. As one of the soldiers was looking down, a large black object appeared in the water under the ice. The object got bigger and bigger. They hadn't made it two steps, when they were all startled by a loud boom. And their world crumbled underneath them.

The submarine had surfaced right where the satellite was sitting. The huge charred chunk of metal was lifted up and then rolled off the side of the conning tower and dropped back down to the ice. The commandos had just cleared the impact zone, but when the submarine hit, it punched a hole right through the ice and sank abruptly. There was complete chaos amongst the commandos. The two that were the closest to the submarine were struggling to hang on to the edge of the ice to stay alive. They also wanted to get the CPU back to CIA headquarters and they struggled with the weight of the unit.

Lieutenant Boxwell was shouting orders.

"Assault team, get those men out of the water. Rocket launcher, punch a hole in the side of that sub. Get a rope down to that CPU and secure it to the chopper."

One of the assualt team commandos tossed a rope down to another commando, who attached it to the CPU, while the first commando tied it to a skid of the helicopter. The two who were in the water were still holding onto the CPU.

"Lift them out," Lieutenant Boxwell shouted to the chopper pilot.

The helicopter started to rise, the rope pulled tight and five commandos were dragged up on the ice and as they became airborne they let go of the line. One by one they dropped down onto the ice. The men were wearing survival suits and they had trained extensively to handle cold.

At the same time the rocket launcher fired not one but two rockets at the tail of the sub. One rocket disabled the tail and the second one missed. Afraid that they were going to lose the opportunity, Boxwell yelled to the comm officer. And the communications officer came running. The special forces team had been accompanied by an AC-130 Specter Gunship and it had been circling the area at 20,000 feet.

Chris Boxwell ordered the Specter Gunship to destroy the sub. The comm officer lit the sub up with a laser that was attached to a box that sent a wireless signal to the Specter Gunship, giving it the exact location of the sub. Bjorn had been kept in the second chopper and as he sat there watching the action, he was transported back to Vietnam. The United States Air Force had just started using the AC-130s in 1968, and Bjorn had seen the devastation they could dole out on ground forces. However, he had never seen it used on a submarine before.

The captain of the submarine frantically began shouting orders.

"Close the door to the engine compartment." And in doing so he doomed six submariners to their death as the engine compartment began filling with water.

"Dive, dive," he shouted.

He knew if he was underwater he would be safe from the assault from above. That would give him some time to figure out the problems with the engine room. But it was not going to work out quite that way.

The Specter Gunship had been patiently circling around the area of the downed satellite for the last hour. Once the coordinates were fixed they began to open up on the hapless sub. The gunship opened up with a barrage of rounds from the 40 mm Gatling gun and the 105 mm cannons. The result was the sub had more holes in it than a block of Swiss cheese, thus ruining any chance of survival for those on board.

Lieutenant Boxwell had cleared the area, because they had escaped with the CPU, which was now dangling under the chopper. And the sub and satellite were headed to the bottom of Hudson Bay, to be recovered at a later time by the Canadian government.

Chris Boxwell and the rest of the Delta Force team made it back to the second chopper, and as the pelting from the Specter began they took off and hovered in the area to make sure the mission was complete. Then they returned to Grand Forks as well.

The satellite had lit up the sky in a color different than that of the northern lights. During the dramatic fall of the satellite, Romy saw the entire thing, and he hitched up Wing Nut and skijored to a hillside overlooking the action. He witnessed everything, including the satellite falling, the submarine, the rocket launcher, the helicopters and the Specter Gunship. None of these he had ever seen before or had any idea of what they meant. As he watched he met up with Sinker and a wounded Ursa. The four of them watched as the events unfolded. And then everything disappeared as if nothing had happened but a large hole in the ice. Romy knew he couldn't take Ursa back to the village.

Romy decided to take Ursa to his father and tell him of all the fascinating things he had just witnessed. But there was no one at the tent camp, so Romy began a new life there and took care of Ursa's wounds. The four of them started a new family.

CHAPTER 34

While keeping her distance from the director of the CIA, Karen sat quietly observing the proceedings in the situation room. She was most interested in the power plays and games that were happening between the characters. However she was very concerned about what was happening six thousand miles away. Typical of most mothers, Karen wanted to protect her young from any threat, even though Luna was twenty-two years old and trying to be independent from her parent. Karen was unsure what these egotistical fools all trying to better the next guy might do.

And Luna was a young girl who was totally unsuspecting of any danger. Karen had had to leave Hawaii so quickly that she was only able to leave Luna a note pinned to her door. Right then and there Karen made herself a promise that she would try and call Luna as soon as it was practical to do so. She slid up her sleeve and glanced at her watch. 3:30 a.m. That would be 9:30 p.m. in Hawaii. *This would be a perfect time to call,* she thought.

"Dr. Harner," the vice president said.

Suddenly Karen realized she was being addressed, but she had been totally disconnected from the conversation.

"Oh, what, I'm sorry, I didn't hear you," she stammered.

"The president just asked you how long it would take for the blackout to reach New York City?" the vice president said.

She looked around the room and everyone was staring at her in silence.

"Ah, I'm sorry, could you repeat the question?"

She inhaled a deep sigh, as the president asked, with a lot of impatience in his voice, "How long will it take the blackout to reach New York City?"

"Well, it took three hours for the blackout to reach Syracuse, so you can extrapolate the time it would take just by calculating the distance from the border to Syracuse and then from Syracuse to New York City."

"I don't want to be taught how to calculate it. I want an answer," the president shouted.

Karen blushed and felt the heat in her face. She glanced at the director of the CIA and received a very hard glare.

"And what is ex . . . trapo . . . whatever?" the president asked, shaking his head.

"Um, it's about the same distance to Syracuse as it is to New York City, so I would estimate about three hours from now."

"So three hours to New York City, it would take a long time for the whole country to go dark," the vice president said.

"Yes, sir," Karen said, then she hesitated, because she didn't want to give them a way out.

"How long?" the president asked, looking at Karen.

"I would have to calculate the distance."

The president rolled his eyes, and Karen wanted to get the hell out of this place. That's when she dropped the bomb she didn't want to drop.

"Excuse me, sir." Everyone in the room looked up.

"Go ahead."

"The blackout may not get past about halfway across the country."

"What's it afraid of, water?" the president said jokingly and looking around the room to garner support. Several of the people laughed to gain support from the president.

"Explain yourself, Miss Harner," the vice president said.

"There is an eastern power grid which takes care of the eastern part of this country. And there is a western power grid which takes care of the western part of the United States and then of course there is a Texan power grid which takes care of, you guessed it, Texas."

All around the room jaws hit the floor. No one saw that coming.

"So this power failure could just end at the Mississippi?" Jay Riley asked.

"Yes, but," she left her sentence hanging.

Everyone in the room waited for the bombshell.

"The eastern part of the United States has definitely been affected. Depending on how strong the CME is, the western power grid may be failing, too. Right now. So both grids could fail at the same time." Karen said with a slow cadence keeping the entire group hanging on every word.

"How would we know?" a General asked.

"First of all the line is not on the Mississippi, it's actually on the Montana/North Dakota border down to the New Mexico/Texas border."

"Yes?" the vice president said.

"It might take a while to find out if there is no power in northern Montana, especially at three in the morning," she replied.

"Call the governor of Montana," the chief of staff whispered to one of his aides.

"Well, Texas will be okay," President Hoaglund said, "My home state. This means we are going to move the Capitol, the White House and everything else, to Texas."

Karen couldn't help shaking her head in disbelief. But one place she knew would be fine was Hawaii because the Hawaiian islands were responsible for their own electrical generation, so this rolling blackout would never affect them. She just didn't know how Luna was doing. She had never really left Luna alone before, but she had to place a call before the power outage hit Washington, D.C. She was getting very anxious.

Conversations went around the room in hyperdrive, as if they had solved the problem, and the grid had not been shut down yet. They completely lost the focus of the best way to deal with the impending disaster and all because of political pressures to keep their party on top.

On the return trip to Grand Forks AFB the helicopters were met by a refueling tanker so they could make the trip back. The pilots looking down as they flew saw total darkness with the exception of the green light coming from the sky. Then they passed over an interstate and saw the line of headlights and suddenly all was right with the world.

Chris Boxwell stared out the side window. Now that the mission was winding down, he could relax some what. But the thought of losing a member of his team weighed heavily on his mind. It wasn't from enemy action and he blamed himself because he should have reminded everyone to hook their static lines into the ring. The mini gun commando had been a friend of his. If there was anything to be happy about, it was that quick thinking had saved five more members of his team when the sub had surfaced.

His gaze moved around the chopper and suddenly he was starring in the eyes of Bjorn Tillson. His eyes were quite different, very vibrant, almost eerie. Chris had learned to read people and in these eyes he saw danger, and an innate sense of confidence.

"What's your name?" he asked.

Bjorn just stared at him, like two warriors facing off.

"Do you have a name?" Chris said again.

"Larry Johns," Bjorn said, using the fictitious name he had taken twenty years ago, his CIA training surfacing.

"Well, Larry, I'm sorry to take you away from your home, but I have my orders."

"I've heard that one before," Bjorn said.

Chris looked closer at the face and thought he saw old scars through the patchy beard. There must be a story here.

I've heard that one before. Definitely military, Chris thought.

Bjorn stared back at him and thought, *It was twenty years ago. He couldn't be onto me.*

"Are you Canadian?"

Bjorn just casually looked back at him with those eyes that would make anyone squirm. *He's fishing,* Bjorn thought. *Well, maybe I'll give him a nibble.*

"Chinese," Bjorn said knowing that the burn had made his eye lids a lot tighter.

Chris chuckled, looking at the beard. *There's more to this story then he is letting on, he thought.*

Bjorn shifted, trying to get comfortable, but the zip tie that bound his hands was starting to get painful and his hands were falling asleep. He knew a lifetime of discomfort; he just had to ignore the hassles. The chopper landed at Grand Forks Air Force Base. The first chopper had already been there for about 30 minutes and there were MPs and medics all over the place. Aleksei and Remus were being treated by the medics, while the bodies of Dimitry and the deceased commando were taken to the morgue.

The medics decided to get the injured men to the clinic at the base and the surviving commandos were taken there also to be sure they had no frostbite and to get some dry clothes. When the second chopper landed, they followed the same course of action. As soon as they were done with the necessary checks, Lieutenant Boxwell ordered the AC-130 fired up and everyone including the body bags were taken out to the runway and loaded onto the transport plane, headed for Andrews Air Force Base in Washington, D.C.

Harlan Mckenzie got the message from a White House aide. He got up and talked to the vice president. Then he kept the promise he had made to Karen. He walked over to her.

"Come with me," he said.

When they walked out of the situation room, he said, "The commando team will be landing at Andrews in a few minutes, so you will be getting your interviews."

"With just the commandos?" she asked, still not trusting the director.

"No, there are three people who aren't commandos," he replied.

"Good," she said.

When they got to Andrews Air Force Base, they were ushered into the place where the AC-130 was taxiing. The ramp at the back of the plane lowered and the commandos carried out the wounded, and they were taken to a nearby hospital. Then two commandos walked down the ramp holding the arms of a man who appeared to be handcuffed. His native clothing had been changed to an orange jump suit so they could be certain there were no weapons. Karen looked at the man with the beard and the disheveled look.

The sky was green but had begun to fade as the Sun came up. Karen looked at the eastern horizon knowing that the flaming orb that would soon appear was the source of all the problems they would face. But she also knew that it had given everything on this planet life. Karen was excited because the information she got from these witnesses could provide her with information that would bring a lot of theories to reality. It was work that she had been doing for over ten years now. She didn't want any disaster to befall anyone, but it was exciting to have her work come to fruition. It was still dark enough that she couldn't see the faces of the people as they disembarked the aircraft.

"Dr. Harner, you will go to the hospital and interview the injured people first, then you can return to CIA headquarters and interview the man there. A CIA agent will take you to the hospital and then bring you to Langley.

"Okay," she said.

"There is at least one person who is a Russian KGB agent. Your questioning will be strictly about the CME, is that clear?"

"Of course," she said.

Bjorn's body suddenly tensed and his mind was squirming like a bag of snakes. He had been thrust into so many emotions so quickly that he lost his typical stoic mindset. So many dominoes were falling around him that it made him catch his breath.

Bjorn recognized the voices around him. The first voice had a thick brogue and he recognized it from the past and he knew immediately that the CIA had found him out and caught up with him.

I can't believe that bastard held a grudge this long, Bjorn thought.

Then Bjorn heard the second voice and was shocked beyond anything he could have anticipated. This voice was one that he never thought he would hear again.

This can't be, the agency drew her into this or did she go on her own. Maybe that wasn't really Karen, he thought. Then someone said Dr. Harner. Doctor? She has really done well for herself. He avoided making eye contact with anyone. Then the male voice kept referring to the CIA.

This couldn't be happening, this must be a dream. The warrior had dozens of thoughts racing through his mind.

Were these really the people from my past? How did we all come together like this? Do they all know the connections like I do? he wondered.

He felt his heart racing in his chest and the commandos moved him through the crowd quickly. Then they took him to the CIA headquarters in Langley, Virginia while an ambulance took Remus and Aleksei to the hospital with the members of the Unit in tow.

CHAPTER 35

"Hello, I'm the agent assigned to help you out," the very nonde-script agent said.

Wow, these agents all look the same. I wonder if they go through some kind of training that makes them all take a similar look. That's makes them very easy to spot, Karen thought.

"Let me guess, your name is Jerry Jones," Karen retorted.

"Yes, how did you guess?" he said, smiling.

"I'm just a mind reader."

"Well, we have a job for you."

"Hey, Agent Jones, when we get to the hospital, I need to make a call."

"That shouldn't be a problem."

The two got into a black sedan and drove to the hospital together. When they arrived, Karen headed to a pay phone and placed a call to her phone in Maui. Luna still lived with her mom because apartments in Maui were far too expensive.

The phone rang and rang without being answered. Karen looked at her watch. It was 6:00 a.m. in Washington, D.C. That meant it was midnight in Hawaii. Karen bit her lip to try to calm her nerves. It was not unheard of for Luna to be out past midnight, but Karen was a little edgy because of the CIA's involvement in this whole thing and the administration's lack of willingness to follow her suggestions.

Where was Luna? Her mind whirled.

Let's see, she could be at her friend's house, she pondered, but Karen didn't have that number with her. *She could be out at a bar,* Karen thought, which any mother hated. But Luna was twenty-two now. And to be honest, Karen had brought this on herself by leaving so quickly. They didn't have too many friends in Maui; it was a hard community to break into. And there were so many tourists that it was hard to connect with the locals.

Then she thought of something. She could call Hoku at the observatory and ask if he could check on her when he left work in the morning. She knew he was a good man. The phone rang and the receptionist picked it up.

"Hello, Mees Observatory."

"May I speak to security, please?" Karen asked.

"Hold, please."

The phone rang in the shed out by the front gate.

"Hello?"

"Hoku?"

"Yes," the burly Hawaiian security guard said.

"Hoku, this is Karen Harner."

"Hello, Miss Karen, where have you been? I haven't seen you."

"I'm in Washington, D.C., talking to the president!"

"Wow, Miss Karen, that is a big deal. I'm impressed," Hoku said.

"Hoku, I need you to do me a favor."

"Yes, ma'am?"

"Would you stop by my house when you leave work in the morning and check on Luna? I haven't been able to reach her and I'm worried."

"Yes, Miss Karen, I will check on Miss Luna."

"Thank you so much, Hoku, and I will call either her or you tomorrow, if the power doesn't go down."

"I am sorry I do not understand. Why the power go down?"

"It's a long story, Hoku. I will give you all the details when I return."

"Okay, bye, Miss Karen."

"Mahalo," Karen said.

"Kipa Mai," Hoku responded.

Karen hung up the phone, not really satisfied, but that was the best she could do. Her eyes stared ahead as she was lost in thought.

The CIA agent was right behind her.

"Doctor?" he said slowly.

She snapped out of her trance.

"Yes, let's go get some work done," she said.

They walked up to Aleksei's room first. Two of the Delta Force commandos were standing guard outside his door. The agent addressed the guards and they let the two in.

There was another commando inside the room.

The man was bruised and battered, but he was awake. He had a very angry look on his face, though.

"There you go, doc, ask away."

Karen nodded at the CIA agent and turned to face the Russian.

"Excuse me, sir, I'm wondering if I could get some information about what you saw last night."

The KGB agent started cursing in Russian.

"Oh well, I guess I'm not going to get any information without a Russian translator," Karen said.

"You have one," the CIA agent said.

"What, you speak Russian?"

He didn't say anything, just sat there nodding.

"Okay, well, let's get started."

"Yes, let's get started," the CIA agent said.

"Can you describe the thickness of the northern lights, and if you saw any swirls or patterns to the lights?"

The agent laughed and translated the sentence that Karen had just given him.

The KGB agent just screamed, "Nyet, nyet, nyet." And that was followed by a barrage of Russian curse words.

"Well," she replied.

"I'm sorry, I'm not going to repeat the things he said about you," the CIA agent said.

"You knew this was going to go nowhere, didn't you?" Karen asked.

"I didn't do anything to the guy."

"Shit," Karen said and walked out of the door.

He followed her out and said, "Well, at least you tried."

"Shut up, Jerry," she said sarcastically.

"Well, maybe you'll have more luck with the next subject."

"You're an asshole," she said.

"So I've been told," he said grinning.

"Well you were told the truth" Karen said.

They walked into Remus's room and there was the same amount of security present. The look on Remus's face was surprising. It was a combination of fear, uncertainty, and confusion. In his world Remus had been confident and in control, and that was a world that most people would feel out of control in. But in the world that most people felt very comfortable in, Remus felt very foreign. But no one in the room realized that Remus had never seen a building as big as this and had only seen electric lights a few times.

But Karen immediately recognized the look of chaos in his eyes, because he was in a world that was totally different to him. It was much as if someone had been abducted by aliens in a spaceship. He didn't know were he was and everyone around him was a stranger. He had no idea what they were going to do to him. He had bad memories of the fight between the opposing factions on the ice. And he was badly wounded during the altercation. To add to everything else, he had an IV started and as he gazed at the fluid leaving the bag, he thought it may be the end of him. The commando had to hold him down during the procedure. Because his left arm was injured, keeping him under control wasn't difficult. To ensure control, his other hand was handcuffed to the bed rail.

When Karen saw that, she thought of her child and demanded that he be released from his bonds. When the commando looked at the CIA agent, she said.

"Jerry, you get the cuffs off this boy."

"Now, why do you need that, Karen?"

"He is still a child, and where are his parents?"

"His father is in custody. You will talking to him in a few minutes."

"Is my dad okay?" Remus blurted out.

"You see, this boy is terrified," Karen said.

"I'm not afraid," Remus retorted.

"I know," Karen said, "you look like a tough guy, but this country has laws which say that you can't hold children without their parents' consent."

"I'm not a child!" he said."

"Look, Remus, am I saying your name right, Remus?"

"Yes, that's my name."

"I have a daughter who's twenty-two years old and she will always be my child."

"Well, my mom died. She died while having my brother and me, that's what my dad said."

"I am so sorry, Remus, that must be so hard for you."

"Well, I never knew her, and my dad teaches me how to take care of myself."

"Where is your brother?"

"I think he is in the village."

"In the Northwest Territories?" she asked with her voice rising.

"I don't know, we just call it the village."

"Is he alone?"

"No, he's with Aga."

"Who's Aga?"

"She lives in the village."

"Oh, okay, so he's being taken care of."

"I guess," Remus said.

"All I mean is, you didn't leave him out in the woods."

He looked at her out of the corner of his eye, trying to figure out where this was going. "No, there are houses in the village."

"How old are you, Remus?" Karen inquired.

"What?" he asked, because he had never talked about age with anyone.

"Do you know how many years have you been alive?"

"A bunch I guess, but what is a year?"

"Okay, well, let me talk to the agent here."

She walked over to "Jerry" and confronted him.

"Are you kidding me?" she said in a hushed voice, "This is like a feral child. You can't be serious about not having his father here. You can't do medical procedures on him."

The CIA agent looked over at the IV line in the boy's arm.

"We can if we had to save his life," the agent whispered. "Now you need to get on with your questions."

She turned back to Remus.

"I'm a scientist, and I need to ask you some questions about the aurora."

Remus just sat there, looking at the woman, who seemed to be speaking a language he wasn't familiar with. But the boy was quick. After all, he could communicate with Romy.

"You are a sci . . . en . . . what?" he asked.

"That means I study the stars."

He flashed a quick smile and said. "I study the stars, too. I know The Seven Sisters, and my favorite, Ursa Major, and a bunch more because my dad says we can see more stars than anyone one else. Ursa is the name of my bear."

"You have a bear?!"

"Yeah, he's a friend of my dad and me, and my brother."

"Great," she said but was thinking, *this is getting stranger by the minute.*

Karen went on to explain everything to him and asked him her basic questions about the northern lights. Remus liked her and became very comfortable in her presence. He was much more comfortable with her than with the guys standing in the room.

CHAPTER **36**

Chris Boxwell and another commando accompanied Bjorn to a side entrance, but they went through the lobby to get to the interrogation room. Bjorn paused as they passed the memorial wall which honored past CIA agents killed in the line of duty. The wall was white tile with black stars. These stars represented deceased agents, but no names were attached to the stars. Bjorn had known of this wall for the last twenty years but had never seen it until now. He stood there for a few minutes, knowing that one of these stars was him. Finally the commando on his left arm said.

"You got a problem?"

"Yeah, one of the stars on this wall is incorrect," Bjorn said.

The two commandos looked at each other and shook their heads. "What are you talking about?" Chris asked.

"I'm still alive," Bjorn returned.

The commandos had picked up this guy in the middle of the Arctic. They thought the cold had affected his mind. Finally they got on an elevator and ascended several floors. When they got out, they walked down a hall to an interrogation room.

One of the commandos stayed inside while Chris walked down the hall to the office of director of the CIA and knocked. Harlan Mckenzie answered the door and Chris said, "One of the subjects from the satellite mission is in the interrogation room. Bjorn's hands were secured behind him and one was attached to the chair.

"You know I'm not sure what you guys were looking for, but you have the wrong man," Bjorn said.

His mind was spinning like a top. So that was Mckenzie's voice he had heard at the airport. He quickly glanced around the room, seeing the one-way glass. But he couldn't see an avenue of escape. Many years ago he had crushed his hand; when it healed it was a little deformed. The hand could be folded into a size the same diameter as his arm. The guard was standing in front of him and said, "Your being here was not my decision. I'm just following orders," the commando said.

While they chatted, Bjorn used his good hand to squeeze and fold his injured hand. With some effort and pain, he slipped it out of the handcuff. But it wasn't the right time to act, so he slipped it back in. Now he knew he had an ace up his sleeve. He also knew he was outnumbered. He had no argument with the commandos, so he decided to wait for the right moment. Chris and Director Mckenzie walked down the hall. Chris asked, "Director, I'm wondering if you knew about that sub?"

The director spun around and gave him an evil stare.

"Of course I did. We pride ourselves on knowing everything."

"Sir, I could have lost five members of my team. Don't you think that information would have been valuable to us?"

"Are you challenging me, lieutenant?"

"Well, if you didn't do your job, I do want an explanation."

"Do you know who you're talking to?"

"The guy who tried to kill five of my guys."

"Look, Lieutenant, there was only one death on this mission and it was one that you could have prevented."

"He reacted too quickly when we saw the satellite falling and thought we were going down, but what I want to know is why you hung us out to dry?"

"Wow, the special forces have certainly changed to a bunch of whiners. I'm going to have a talk with the general who oversees your unit because let's face it, these decisions are made at a level much higher than yours."

"Yes, but when these decisions threaten the lives of my men, I want answers!"

"Come on, Lieutenant, you have a job which could take your life. Every one of your men accepts that that risk."

"Yes, but when your own team is working against you, it's my job to make things right."

Chris Boxwell clenched his teeth to keep his anger under control. He had times when he wanted to punch someone and this was one of those times. But if he let his anger control him, he would most certainly lose his career.

Harlan Mckenzie was put off by this subordinate challenging him and decided to skip going to the one-way glass window. Instead he went right into the interrogation room to interview this backwoods hillbilly. As Director Mckenzie entered the room, he turned to Chris and said, "Your job here is done, you can return to Fort Bragg."

Chris walked down the hall and was followed by the other commando.

The director gave a signal to security and an officer joined him in the room. The door entered on the left side of Bjorn and he was looking straight ahead. Harlan Mckenzie walked to the head of the table and sat down. He looked at the disheveled man with the patchy blonde beard. The man looked back and Harlan froze for a second. The man was vaguely familiar. Then he looked at those eyes. Bjorn's eyes had darkened a bit but they still had that blue-green hue.

Director Mckenzie had been trained to hide emotion but tingles went down his spine as Bjorn looked at him with all the confidence he ever had. The face in front of him was unexpected and he wasn't sure, so he asked, "What is your name, sir?"

"I want to see my son," Bjorn replied.

"Your son is being taken care of in the hospital."

Bjorn recognized the face in front of him even though it was twenty years older. He felt his molars clench and his jaw muscles flex as his eyes burned into the embodiment of evil in front of him. He felt an intense hatred for the man that he thought he was rid of many years ago. Finally he had an opportunity to end this hatred that had built up in him for the last twenty years. The two men were frozen in time. Neither of them knew what to say, and a staring match ensued.

The director tried to diffuse the tension in the room.

"My old friend," he said, laughing a very manufactured laugh.

"You have no friends here," Bjorn said barely releasing the tension on his teeth.

The guard in the room, sensing the tension, immediately became more vigilant.

"If you cooperate with us, you will get to see your son a lot quicker."

"I won't cooperate till I see my son."

Director Mckenzie stood up and walked out of the room. He needed some time to think. He walked into the room with the one-way glass. He gazed into the eyes of his one-time nemesis, which he had thought he was rid of. Bjorn estimated the position of a person on the other side of the glass and locked his gaze right into Harlan's eyes. Bjorn Tillson. So he didn't die in that napalm attack, but he must have just barely escaped, judging by the facial scars. He must have had his face bandaged if he was in the MASH unit back in Vietnam and probably switched dog tags with a dead soldier.

That is the last thing I need right now. Tillson was the only one left who knew about the drug program back in the sixties, Mckenzie thought. *This could end my career with the CIA, and I was going to retire in the next ten years.*

He couldn't stand looking into those eyes anymore, so he walked back to his office to think this over.

This is an unexpected bump in the road. Now I need to figure out a way to deal with this and make it right. Tillson's death would go unnoticed on the streets of D.C. His family and everyone who knew him thought that he had died in Vietnam. Let's see, he probably lived a solitary life up in Canada. Since he wasn't needed for this investigation, they could just release him and then somehow some gang members would have a disagreement with him on the mean streets of D.C., the director thought.

Harlan picked up the phone to see if he could set something up and hopefully save his career. Karen had finished her interview with Remus. She and her CIA shadow arrived at CIA headquarters. When she walked into the interrogation room, the CIA agent named "Jerry" said to the guard, "Hey, I have to hit the can, you got this?"

"Well, I'd appreciate it if you just used the can and not hit it." Both men shared a chuckle. Then "Jerry" disappeared down the hall.

Karen walked around to the head of the table and sat down, facing her last interview in this strange episode. She organized her papers and as she was shuffling the stack, she said, "Hi, my name is Karen Harner. I'm a solar astronomer studying the northern lights."

Bjorn's heart nearly stopped, and then it was beating so hard and fast that he wondered if it was going to jump out of his chest. Karen then looked up at her interviewee and her mouth dropped open as she looked at the man and then at his eyes. He looked back at her. She didn't know what to say. The beard was a little confusing and the scars were even more disturbing.

"Um, ah, um," her voice stuttered as she tried to compose herself.

"Um, what's your name, sir?" she said as her voice quivered.

His eyes had always made her melt along with his blonde hair. Although it was a bit messy, she still wanted to run her fingers through it.

"My name is Larry Johns," he said, because the officer was still in the room and he was sure they were being recorded.

"Oh, I'm sorry, you look like a friend of mine," she said, regaining her composure. She shook her head.

The resemblance is amazing, she thought. She looked over at Larry Johns and those eyes captivated her again, but as she looked at them again, they were tearing up.

"Are you okay?" Karen asked. Then, as the two ex-lovers tried to find their next words, the lights went out.

The officer walked out of the dark office to see what the problem was. The power came back on as the emergency generator fired up. However, the generator was old and the maintenance had been neglected. The pistons seized up and the metal fused into itself. The lights went out again.

Bjorn looked around, trying to see in the dark room and to figure out what was going on. He quickly slipped his bad hand out of the hand cuff, and was free. Karen knew exactly what was going on; the power outage that she had been predicting had arrived.

They felt their way around the room. Suddenly they realized they were touching each other. Karen's hair tingled because this man, whoever he was, looked like her ex-boyfriend and his strong arms felt very familiar. Her hand slipped into that beautiful hair. Then their arms were tight around each other, and their lips were suddenly locked together. Then she knew that this was Bjorn, because she had only been kissed like this once before in her life.

"You are Bjorn," she said as she grabbed his shirt.

He pulled her close and whispered in her ear.

"You have to whisper because there are recording devices in this room," he said, then said, "Hi Karen, been a long time."

"Why did you lie to me?"

"I didn't lie to you. I was lying to the CIA."

"I can't believe you are alive."

"We are in grave danger. We need to get out of here," he whispered in her ear.

"Are you in trouble?" she asked.

"I will be if I stay here," he said.

The power failure had caused the power door locks to fail. So they simply turned the door knob and stepped out into the hallway. The hallway was lit by battery-powered emergency lights. Karen was

not accustomed to trembling but she was quivering like a cold puppy. This was a dream that she had thought of many times, and at
the same time it was a very dangerous situation. But right then she
decided to help Bjorn in any way that she could. She was not going
to lose him again.

CHAPTER **37**

They slipped their shoes off to walk quietly down the hallway. Soon they heard voices coming from another hallway and they quickened their pace. Karen and Bjorn eventually got to the emergency stairwell and closed the door quietly behind themselves. It was just in time, because the guard and Director Mckenzie walked into the interrogation room, and finding it empty, ran out and sounded the alarm. By then the two fugitives were at an emergency exit and Karen directed him to the car that she and "Jerry" had arrived in, and a quick look around produced a key.

Bjorn started the car but then on second thought, he said, "Why don't you drive. I haven't been in a car in fifteen years."

They switched positions and she quickly headed for the hospital where Remus was.

"Is Remus really your son?"

"He is," Bjorn replied.

"You should be very proud, he is very polite, and a strapping young man," she said smiling.

"Thanks."

"Where's your wife?"

"Well, we were never really married and then she died in childbirth."

"Oh, no, I am so sorry."

"Yeah, when you live in the Northwest Territories and the shit hits the fan, you can only depend on yourselves. I blame myself."

"Are you a doctor?"

"No."

"So how can you blame yourself?"

"People always relied on me in tough situations, but I totally failed on this one."

"Wow, I think you are being too hard on yourself."

"Maybe, but I'm alive and she's dead. The boys will never know what it's like to have a mother."

"How did she die?"

"She just kept bleeding after the birth, but it was slow bleeding, nothing dramatic, so I thought it would eventually stop."

"So postpartum hemorrhage."

"If you say so, I was never really trained in medical care. Do you have any children?" Bjorn asked.

Karen hesitated and looked out the window, trying to stop her tears.

"Yes, I have a daughter," she said.

"And your husband is probably a very intelligent scientist, like you."

"Well, he was very intelligent. But now I'm divorced. His intelligence got in the way of love. And he came to the conclusion we would be better off splitting up."

"Who would be crazy enough to leave you?"

"He decided he couldn't live with me."

Are you kidding me?"

She thought that he must not remember, but she was happy when they pulled into the parking lot of the hospital because she didn't want to answer that rhetorical question.

They stepped out of the car and the sky was still a light green color.

"Bjorn, do you remember that night in Michigan before you left when we saw the northern lights?"

"Do I remember? One of the biggest mistakes I've ever made, but now I have a chance to make it right, if that's what you want."

Karen smiled. "Remember, I said it looked like the sky is bleeding?"

"Yes, and with everything that's happened in my life, I wish I could go back to that simpler time."

"You will have to catch me up on everything that has happened to you."

"Sure, but now we still have that problem with the CIA," he said.

"And how are we going to get into the hospital and past the guards?"

"I'm having chest pain."

"What?" Karen said with a lot of concern in her voice.

"You have to play along," he said, smiling.

"Oh, I get it," she said.

Karen gave him her jacket and then they walked through the doors of the emergency room, Karen under his arm and Bjorn limping a little. Luckily it was a busy night in the ER. Because Bjorn was complaining about chest pain he was put in a room immediately. As soon as they entered the room Bjorn closed the door. Behind the door two white lab coats were hanging.

"Perfect," Bjorn said.

The doctor came into the room quickly after hearing "chest pain"; it had become one of the "big five" medical complaints in the modern era. After the doctor left, Bjorn quickly went to the storage cabinet, got a pair of scissors and a razor and hacked and shaved his beard off. Karen trimmed his hair to a respectable length. When Karen saw the new Bjorn she was shocked. She began to see the young Bjorn. Then Bjorn shoved several pillows under the blanket of the bed. They put on the lab coats When the X-ray tech came in to do a portable X-ray, they said, "We'll step out during this procedure."

The X-ray tech nodded.

Remus was in Room 502 and Karen led the way to the fifth floor. As they walked down the hall towards the room, Bjorn stopped in front of another room and pulled the chart out of the rack by the door. He spoke quietly to Karen as they stood there as if they were discussing a case. But Bjorn was skilled at observing his environment. He saw the guard down the hall and he even spotted the fire alarm on the wall. They walked down to it and he positioned Karen between the fire alarm and the guard. He quickly reached up and pulled the alarm.

The guard disappeared, looking for the emergency. Karen and Bjorn slipped into Remus's room.

"Hi, Karen," the boy said. Then he did a double take, barely recognizing the man with her.

"Hi, son," Bjorn said.

"Dad?!" Remus said.

"Everybody in the bathroom," Bjorn said.

"What?" Remus and Karen asked.

"We have to make a plan."

The three of them crowded into the bathroom with the IV stand. When they were all in there, Bjorn locked the door.

"Dad, what did you do?" Remus asked.

"Remus there are some bad people looking for me, from my past, so I had to change my appearance."

"What bad people?" Remus asked, while Karen hung on every word.

"It's a long story and I will explain everything to you when I have time."

Remus looked at his father and then his gaze went to Karen. She was nodding and then said, "Listen to your dad. He knows what he's doing."

CHAPTER **38**

Director Mckenzie was beside himself with anger as he gazed upon his nemesis for twenty years. And especially since he thought the guy had been eliminated from the face of the Earth, this was the kind of surprise he didn't want. And how did he draw this astrophysicist into his lair, in less than a day. Harlan saw himself as the best thing the CIA had ever known and an attractive chunk of manhood. But he couldn't explain the attraction to Tillson this gorgeous woman felt. She was with a guy who would make a Neanderthal look good.

He made sure that his agents stayed at the headquarters, so he could take care of this problem once and for all, without any witnesses.

Let's see, where would they go? Oh yeah, his son. I'm sure he is the rescuer that he always was. This will be easy, he thought.

Mckenzie drove to the hospital. Karen and Bjorn had just arrived in the room and they were talking to Remus in the bathroom. When Mckenzie got to Room 502 he opened the door with a gun in his hand. The room was empty but there was light coming out from under the bathroom door. Harlan walked to the door and knocked.

"Hello, this is Director Mckenzie. I'm with the CIA."

Karen's body immediately tensed, and her eyes got as big as saucers, even though she knew the guy and had stood her ground with him on several occasions. Still the guy had always made her feel on edge, and now she knew why.

"Tell him you are using the bathroom," Bjorn whispered in his son's ear.

"I'm busy in the bathroom," Remus shouted at the closed door.

"No problem, I'll wait," the director replied.

Bjorn's mind quickly went into high speed mode. They were unarmed and Bjorn knew that Mckenzie would be armed. He whispered instructions to Remus and Karen. Remus slowly opened the door while Bjorn and Karen hid behind it.

"Hi, Remus," Mckenzie said with a pleasant voice, as if he was an old friend.

But Remus had never met the guy before.

"I don't know you," Remus said

"I'm a friend of your dad."

"Okay."

"Hey, have you heard from or seen your dad?"

Remus suddenly became silent. He looked at Mckenzie and his eyes quickly flashed to the bathroom door and back to the director. It was only for a fraction of a second but Mckenzie knew—he was experienced at reading the human face. Remus slowly walked back to the bed with his rolling IV pole.

"No, I haven't seen him."

Mckenzie reached under his jacket and pulled out a 9 mm pistol.

"Tillson, it's over."

Remus stopped and turned back to face the director. He couldn't lose his father and he felt he had done something wrong. Bjorn knew he had to get into this fray. But first he held up his index finger to his lips and looked at Karen. She nodded her head.

Bjorn stepped out to face his arch enemy.

"So where is your girlfriend?" Harlan said with the gun leveled on Bjorn.

"Ha, ha," Bjorn laughed and said, "I haven't had a girlfriend for twenty years."

"You know who I mean. Where's the astrophysicist?"

"I have no idea who you're talking about."

"Okay, the first thing I'm going to do is a double tap in the chest of your son, there. Will that help your memory?"

Karen couldn't take it anymore; she couldn't stay hiding in the bathroom and let the man of her dreams and his son die. Karen stepped out of the bathroom.

"Wow, the whole crew is here, what luck! So Dr. Harner, I knew you were trouble from the start. What the hell do you see in this guy? I mean look at his face, and by the way, that was a gift from me to your boyfriend. Do you approve?"

She was scared and shocked that she was in this scene that was straight out of Hollywood.

"Mr. Mckenzie, please don't do this. Bjorn and I grew up together twenty years ago. And you ask what I see in him, well, that can't be seen."

"Oh, I get it. You are childhood sweethearts. How the hell did I get this unlucky, that I found your old girlfriend and brought her back to you?" Mckenzie asked, laughing.

"Mckenzie, take me. These two don't know anything," Bjorn said.

"Don't know anything about what? The juice program, as you used to call it? And if you would have gone along with the program, we would have won that damn war, and you would have been a fuckin' superman."

"Yeah, but research showed that that shit killed a lot of my friends. These two have no interest in a problem that happened twenty years ago, so let them go!"

"Yeah, but this is complicated, Bjorn. I could just cuff these two to the bed and you and I could go for a walk outside. But come on, you and I know that they will be on the phone as soon as we leave," Harlan said.

"So what are you going to do, you going to kill all of us?"

"Well, Bjorn, you put me in this position. Any other options will trash my career and probably put me in jail for the rest of my life, especially with that bullshit about your 'juice.'"

Harlan was standing with his back toward the door and he had his gun down at his waist. Bjorn was trying to think of a way to get the gun from him. Karen, Bjorn and Remus were standing against the wall. It was a private room because Remus and Aleksei were under guard until the fire alarm went off and the guard left to investigate. Now the three of them were in the room with a man with a gun and a very bad attitude. There was only one person in the room that was as calm as if he did this every day. And of course Mckenzie knew that his first bullet would have to go there.

Then something happened that no one expected, and one person didn't see coming.

The rolling power failure continued heading south, totally encompassing the city of Washington, D.C. The nation's capital went dark, with everything north of the city also powerless. Emergency power kicked on at the White House and worked without lapse.

At the situation room total havoc had begun to take over, as everyone in there tried to come up with a way to slow and even halt the inevitable blackout. The governors of at least thirteen states had been calling, demanding answers. The vice president was fielding most of those calls. The president was becoming more and more disoriented by the lack of sleep and everybody screaming for answers.

"Look, everyone, we have decided that shutting the power grid down would be more devastating than just riding this out," President Hoaglund said.

"No, you are just trying to protect your own political campaign," a congressman from New York, seeking answers for his state, shouted.

"That's not true, I have a plan if the whole country goes dark," the president replied.

"What's your plan?"

"We will move the capital to Texas, because Texas is safe."

The members of the administration were slinking away from the president as a lot of moaning and shouting began to erupt from the members of his own administration.

People around the Northeast began to panic, especially as night began to fall again. They were swarming stores to stock up on supplies. The first items to disappear were batteries and flashlights; those items became completely unavailable throughout a large area.

Bjorn was giving the CIA director a hard stare; his only desire was to take the life of this man. He was standing in front of Karen and Remus. He had a realization that he was there with the love of his life. In addition to that there was his son, who had developed into a solid young man and didn't deserve this fate. Neither of them should have been here in this time with these people.

CHAPTER **39**

The commando team was stuck at Langley until the morning because the rolling power outage had grounded all the flights into and
out of Washington, D.C. Chris Boxwell and a couple of the commandos were sitting in a dark hotel room discussing the mission. They
were using their night vision goggles to see each other. The rest of
the team had gone downstairs to the restaurant to get some food and
alcohol now that the mission had come to an end. The restaurant was
using candles to give their patrons light because they had no choice
and the manager hoped it would add some ambience to the whole
crisis. One of the commandos mentioned that Larry Johns had spent
some time in the military and he just sensed it from the man. Chris
Boxwell agreed that he had picked up those signals, too.

The commander of the team decided that since he had nothing
else to do, he would go find out where those scars had come from and
the story behind this guy. He took a cab over to the CIA headquarters
in Langley. The building was darker than it should be and when he
checked in with a guard, he found out that the disheveled man and
Karen had walked out of the place when the power went out. That
was even more interesting than all the other craziness that was happening now.

Who was this guy? he thought. *He must have gone to the hospital to get his son, but what are they running from?* he wondered. *I have got to meet this guy and hear his story.*

He walked into the hospital right behind Director McKenzie and asked for the room of Remus Tillson. The nurse said, "Wow, that patient is popular tonight."

Chris wondered what that meant but it must be because his dad was here. The nurse told him Room 502. When he walked up to the room, he found the door was opened about six inches. He heard voices and at least one of them sounded very threatening. Lieutenant Boxwell stood out of sight and took in the conversation. Bjorn was trying to rationalize, and Karen was pleading. But mostly the director of the CIA sounded threatening and it seemed to be something from the Vietnam conflict. Something that he was trying to hide from the Vietnam era.

What was the juice? he wondered. He had to get to the bottom of this, but he wasn't exactly getting along with the director right now.

"Okay, friends, here's what we are going to do. First of all, Karen, you are going to remove the IV from Remus's arm, because that would attract a little too much attention," Mckenzie said.

"But wait a minute, he needs that fluid, damn it," Bjorn chided.

"I'm not sure any of you need anything right now, except to do what I'm telling you."

"What are you planning, you prick?"

"Oh, come on, Bjorn, we are just going to go for a walk. That will be good for him."

"Well, let me get him a wheelchair," Bjorn said.

"No, Remus is going to walk with me and if anybody does anything that I don't like, Remus is going to suffer, a lot."

Chris Boxwell recognized the name and remembered a press release from many years ago and it was basically about an operative that had virtually started the Delta Force and clandestine operations way back in the Vietnam conflict. But there was something dirty here and it involved the director, too. He had heard enough, he had to act. He moved silently and got down on his knees and took a quick look inside the room from the bottom of the door frame. He was trying to find out where everybody was located in the room. Bjorn, who was facing the door noticed the quick flash of a human face at the bottom of the door, and knew something was about to go down.

"Okay, Karen, you got that IV out of his arm," Mckenzie said.

"Yes," Karen replied as she ground her teeth together.

"Okay, Remus, just walk over here."

Chris moved quickly and quietly. He slipped one arm around Mckenzie, pinning the gun arm against his body. At the same time Bjorn dove and swung at the gun, knocking it down to the floor. Then Lieutenant Boxwell took the thumb and index finger of his other hand and clamped them around the director's trachea. He put firm pressure into the man's neck, effectively stopping any blood flow through the carotid arteries and on to the brain. The commando knew he would lose consciousness in about thirty seconds, and if he released the pressure at that time, Harlan Mckenzie would slowly regain consciousness.

To make things happen a little quicker he squeezed the director's trachea, preventing any sound from being emitted and limiting the amount of air it could carry. Chris caught him as the man's knees buckled. Bjorn stepped forward and lifted the man's legs and the two men laid him on the bed.

Then Bjorn looked Chris dead in the eyes and the unspoken words that special forces commandos often had were out there.

What are we going to do now?

Chris quickly said, "I heard of your history in the last war, and I had to come shake your hand."

Bjorn was stunned. Nobody had ever wanted to be anywhere near him. For someone to say that was totally unheard of. Bjorn extended his hand and Chris grabbed it, and both men could feel the strength in the grip of the two warriors.

"What are you going to do now?"

"I'm not going to do anything, and what you do, I didn't see and I know nothing."

Karen was still stunned and amazed at all of this that had happened right in front of where they were standing. She watched as the commando slipped out the door.

"Well, he's going to wake up in a minute," Bjorn said.

The other two just stood there waiting for someone to make a decision, unsure of the consequences. Bjorn decided he would have to end this once and for all. After all, the guy was going to kill all of them. He quickly grabbed the needle that Karen had removed from Remus's arm. Then he exposed Director Mckenzie's arm and inserted the needle into the vein in his elbow. Bjorn was experienced at this from his drug abuse days. Then he took the scissors out of his pocket and cut the tubing at about two feet. The normal saline solution drained onto the floor.

"Why don't you two walk out into the hallway?" Bjorn said.

"No," Karen said, "I'm going to take responsibility for this as well, but, Remus, you should wait for us in the hallway. Remus grudgingly stepped out of the room.

"You know, if I don't do this, I will never have a day of rest in my life. He will hunt me to the ends of the Earth."

Karen was nodding. Bjorn inhaled deeply, and then he picked up the cut end of the IV line and raised it to his lips. He exhaled all of his air into the tube. The air embolism caused Harlan Mckenzie's body to shut down. An air bubble lodged in his brain and caused a massive stroke. Then another large bubble stopped in his heart and he went into cardiac arrest. Suddenly the world was a better place.

But now the three were fugitives on the run. Bjorn removed the needle from the vein and laid it on the bedside table.

CHAPTER **40**

Aleksei saw a rooster strutting around a barnyard, but the face on the rooster was the face of the captain of the sub. And the rooster was smoking a cigar. This was not normal and he shook his head to clear it. As he woke up in a fog, he looked up at the tile squares of the suspended ceiling. The lines were a little wavy, but with a lot of concentration he got them to straighten out.

When he looked around the room, it was empty and he needed to move around and stretch his body. As he swung his legs off the bed, his head started spinning. In fact, the entire room was spinning around him. He grabbed wildly for something to stabilize himself and his hand hit the side rail on the bed and he held it close to control the dizziness. Eventually he got the spinning under control.

He stood up and took his tentative first steps and soon was walking normally. He opened the door of his room. There was a bustling nurses' station at the end of the hallway. But his Room 501 was in a pod with three other rooms.

He didn't want to go down to the nurses' station, and to his surprise he didn't have much pain. The morphine was actually doing him a world of good, especially with pain reduction. However the delusions were another thing, but if he was awake they weren't that bad.

Aleksei looked at the door of the other rooms and 502 was open partway. He pushed it open and there was a sleeping man on the bed, but the man was fully dressed.

Maybe I could take this guy's clothes and get out of this place, the KGB agent thought.

As he walked up beside the bed he stepped in some water. He looked down to see what he was stepping in. When Aleksei lowered his head, the profound vertigo came back with a vengeance. He tried to stabilize himself, but his feet slipped on the wet floor, as if he was standing on ice. The KGB agent's head flew back as he fell and hit the corner of the bedside table. Then he came to a rest slumped on the floor beside the bed.

A vessel in his cranium started bleeding after his head struck the table. The guard came back to the pod he was supposed to be watching when the fire alarm was under control. He looked in Room 501 and the room was empty.

"Oh, shit," he said as he ran down to the nurses' station.

"Can I help you?" the head nurse inquired, noticing that the guard had a look of guilt and fear on his face.

"I need you to call the police. The prisoner in 501 is on the loose." The nurse turned to another person and said, "Page a code orange, missing person."

Then she ran down the hall with the guard as the announcement transmitted overhead.

"Is 502 okay?" she said as they ran.

"I don't know, I just checked 501," he said as they entered Room 501. The room was still vacant.

Then they looked in 502 and saw the two bodies. The veteran nurse walked in and could immediately tell they were both dead, mostly by the color of their faces. Both men had a very bluish hue to their faces. She checked for a pulse in their necks. As her fingers touched the necks of the men, she searched for a pulse but couldn't find one. A puddle of blood had formed under the head of Aleksei. She walked to the phone on the wall.

"Code Blue, times two, Room 502," she said.

Then she began the required CPR, even though she knew they had been dead for at least thirty minutes and there was no chance of reviving these two patients. The room quickly filled with people of all disciplines in the hospital. To no avail though.

CHAPTER 41

Karen and Bjorn were still in their lab coats and Remus in a pair of disposable scrubs, as they all slowly walked out of the hospital. As they walked out the front door, they heard a lot of excitement going on and then increased the pace.

"What do we do now?" Karen asked.

"I saw a bus station, let's get on a bus and get out of here."

"Yeah, but where are we going, what direction?"

"Good question, let's just find a motel and talk about this."

The authorities were much too busy with the power outage to even notice the three walking down the street. In less than three blocks they passed a motel and Karen walked in to check into a room. Remus had been sutured in the emergency room and with an incredibly busy day he was very tired. He laid down on one of the beds and was soon asleep.

Karen and Bjorn just looked at each other in the stale-smelling motel room. Karen started to cry as she was finally able to relax, and let the tensions of the day and her life flow out of her. Bjorn walked over to her and gave her a big hug.

Her stress and frustrations overflowed and she said, "You left my life in tatters when you walked away from me."

"I know," Bjorn said, his eyes cast down. "And as you can see, that was a huge mistake on my part, but I thought I was doing the right thing."

Bjorn was also tearing up, an act he was not used to, but this was a moment he had dreamed of many times, and with Mckenzie around, he was afraid it was going to be snatched away from him before he could do anything about it. Karen was such a beautiful woman he almost felt he didn't deserve her.

When he kissed her, both of them felt their lips tingling, a feeling she hadn't experienced in a long time. It had been years since she had a real man in her arms, and they had leapt over so many hurdles. She couldn't believe this was happening. As the passion started to build up, she put a flat hand on his chest.

"Wait," she whispered softly, "We need to get to know each other again before the intimacy begins. Plus Remus is here and I wouldn't be comfortable with that."

Bjorn walked away from her with his head in his hands to quell the desire. It had been so very long for him, and he was on fire. Then he shook his head and walked back to her.

"Of course, you are right," he sat down on the bed and she sat down beside him with their backs against the headboard. What ensued was a five-hour conversation about everything that had happened in both of their lives. But Karen left out one little detail, she wasn't ready to reveal.

"Isn't it crazy that we are reunited during one of the most massive solar storms? As I said, it is our destiny."

"Well, let's live it out then."

"So where should we go from here?" she asked.

"Well, I for one don't want to lose you again, and I am pretty sure you are not going to want to live in a tent in the frozen north."

"Have you ever been to Hawaii?"

Bjorn's jaw dropped open.

"Ah, um, ah," he was speechless. Karen was waiting, but to ease his angst she started giggling at him. Then as he blushed, the tension was broken.

"No, yes, no, ah, I mean, oh shit." Bjorn spit out.

Karen's giggling escalated to laughing. She leaned forward and gave him a very gentle kiss. Bjorn was shaking his head in embarrassment.

"Okay," she said. "Let's try again, have you been to Hawaii?"

"It's a difficult question, because, yes, I've been to Hawaii, for about an hour on a military transport. But no I haven't been there like most people go there."

"Well, you and Remus should go there with me," she said.

"There is one problem," Bjorn said. Karen sat there in silence waiting for the other shoe to drop.

"Yes?" she inquired.

"At some point I'm going to have to get back to the Territories and check on Romy, but I'm sure Aga is taking good care of him."

"Okay, well look, because of the power outage, there will be no flights for awhile, so we should start driving or bussing to L.A. That way we can get there ahead of the collapsing power grid."

"But we can't take the CIA vehicle. They will be looking for it."

"No problem we can rent a car. That will be a quicker way to get there."

"We should get some sleep, if we are going to drive."

CHAPTER 42

The drive to L.A. actually took four days because Bjorn didn't have a driver's license and they thought that if they had gotten stopped by the authorities, everything would go down the drain. Remus had never been in a car before much less drive one. They were, after all, fugitives on the run and the CIA was looking for them, as well as every law enforcement agency in the country. Karen stopped at a convenience store and when she came out, she had three boxes of hair dye. She became a blonde and the two men became dark haired. When they stopped at a motel that night they did the deed, and although it took some convincing to get Remus to do it, eventually he acquiesced.

The next day at another stop Karen had a look of urgency on her face as she exited the store. She had a newspaper in her hand and when she got into the car, she handed it to Bjorn. He looked at her, trying to read her expression, then he opened the paper and read:

DIRECTOR OF THE CIA FOUND

DEAD WITH DEAD KGB AGENT

The rest of the article went on with details about the murder. And of course information about the two men involved and a mostly sterling history of Director Mckenzie's life.

"Are we off the hook?" Bjorn asked.

"Apparently. I don't know how that KGB agent got involved, but if that absolves us then all the better."

"But are they still looking for us?"

"Maybe the director of the CIA had a secret he was trying to hide and kept us in the shadows too," Karen stated.

"Well, we can't be too sure about that."

"That reminds me. You should get rid of that gun; it's the last thing that ties you to that guy."

When they crossed over a large lake, Bjorn looked in his rearview mirror and seeing no other traffic in either direction, he rolled his window down and tossed the gun over the rail and into the lake. The next day they rolled into Los Angeles and returned the car at the airport. Then Karen purchased three tickets to Maui, Hawaii.

"So are we going to a tropical paradise?" Bjorn asked.

"Most people consider it a tropical paradise. To be honest with you, it's a very special place but it has its own problems. It's a workplace for me, so I see it differently than most."

"I know you have told me the basic things that you do, but tell me more about your work."

"Well, I work at the Mees Observatory, and I'm an astrophysicist studying solar astronomy. I was called to Washington when this solar storm started, and I tried to save this country from all its hardships but the administration wouldn't go for it. The result is what we have been witnessing. It will take a year to repair all the systems required to run the power grid like we are used to. But the good news is Hawaii has its own power generation. We don't depend on anyone else."

"Why is this observatory on Hawaii?"

"We have the most cloudless days of any place in the United States."

"Wasn't this place a leper colony?"

"No, that's the next island to the west, it's called Molokai. That was a horrible time in the history of the country, a lot like the power outages are causing now. But back in the 1800s people became afraid of leprosy so the people afflicted with that disease were ostracized from society and shipped to Molokai. They were told to survive, if they could."

As Bjorn thought about his own life, he could relate. He was ridiculed and rejected because of a disfiguring injury.

"Well, I'd fit right in there."

Karen smiled at him and said. "Sweetie, people are very critical about themselves, but your scars aren't that bad. Now I'm not downplaying the suffering you have gone through, but your personality shines through your injury and besides they cured leprosy a long time ago. So you wouldn't fit in there. And if your scars are bothering you, I have a friend on Oahu who's a plastic surgeon. Why don't you talk to him?"

"Is this an old boyfriend of yours?"

"No, but his wife is a friend of mine."

"Maybe I'll check it out." Then he reached over and took her hand in his. Time passed on the flight to Hawaii and Karen had time to think. She leaned forward to look at Remus and he was asleep. She turned towards Bjorn. He was as gentle a man as he had always been, despite the fact that he had to do some bad things to save their lives. She was sure she would have done the exact same things.

"Is something bothering you?" she said.

"Just all these changes, and now I'm taking Remus to Hawaii."

"Are you regretting your decision?"

"Well, when we first started off we didn't have a choice, we were trying to survive," he said.

"And now?"

"Now I'm getting to know you again."

"And what do you think?"

"This has been such an amazing event and then all the bumps in the road. I'm just worried about putting my heart out there and then the bottom dropping out again."

"Trust me, I've known that feeling. I have had my trials and tribulations with love in my life, and I thought I would never find true love again."

"Have you?"

"Look, Bjorn, this is our destiny, like I told you many years ago. When I thought you had died, a part of me died, too. But I didn't want to give up, so I kept a part of you in my heart. And even though it was silly, I hoped you would rise from the dead."

"Well, don't start calling me Jesus."

"And now you have risen in a sense. You are back in my arms, and I'm going to raise a white flag and surrender when I know you are this close."

He looked at her with those emerald eyes and she started crying. His hand reached over and pulled her head close to his as she continued quietly sobbing.

"Don't worry, I will be with you till the end of time," Bjorn whispered.

The flight attendant made the announcement that they were landing. Remus started stirring and they took the necessary steps for the end of the flight. Once they had collected the few things that Karen had brought with her she called for a cab. The cab delivered them to Karen's house. Karen sighed as she walked into her sanctuary and she welcomed the two men in. When she walked into the kitchen, there was a note on the table.

Mom, where are you? Hoku came down and told me you were doing okay. But come on, two weeks!? Anyway, I'm surfing in my usual spot. Love, Luna.

"Come on, you guys, I want to introduce you to my daughter."

They drove down to the beach where Luna typically surfed. They parked and walked down to the beach. They saw a couple girls surfing and one of them was wearing a pink bikini. Karen waved. Luna waved back but she wondered who the strange guys were with her mom. She caught the next wave and came running up the beach. Her mom gave her a big hug and apologized effusively and then said.

"Honey, I want you to meet some friends of mine."

Bjorn immediately noticed the bluish eyes as she said, "Okay."

Karen pointed to Remus and said, "Luna, I want to introduce you to your half brother."

The impact of that statement was so powerful you could have knocked every one of them over with a feather. The men and Luna

looked at each other with utter confusion. The realization slowly began to set in.

First Bjorn shook his head and his eyes blinked as he put the back
of one hand up to wipe his eyes. Karen had a silly, secretive grin on
her face as she watched the reactions.

"What?!" Luna exclaimed as she came to the same realization.

"I don't understand," Remus said.

"Mom, are you kidding me! This is my brother?"

By this time Karen was weeping. She nodded to her daughter.

"When did you have him? I thought I was your only child," Luna
said as she dropped her surf board.

"Honey, he's not my son."

The younger people were confused again, but slowly they looked
back and forth around the group, they figured the riddle out. Luna
looked at Bjorn and saw his eyes.

"No, Mom, why did you do this to me, how could you tell me my
dad was dead and then show up with him on this beach."

"Honey, come here." Then Karen brought her into a hug.

Luna couldn't take her eyes off Bjorn.

"Look, everybody. We all just found out about this, so nobody
was keeping any secrets," Karen said in her own defense. Bjorn
looked at her from the corner of his eye and she avoided his questioning glance.

"Well, since you are the only one that knows everything, let's sit
down and have a talk," Bjorn said.

The group all settled down and Karen started talking. "Okay, it's hard to know where to start, so I guess I'll start from the beginning." She looked at Bjorn and said, "You remember when you said you were being deployed to Vietnam. And I won't be too descriptive but I'm sure you remember that night, because I certainly do."

"But you told me you were on birth control."

"I was, but I had just started it, so I guess it hadn't taken effect yet."

"So why did you wait until now to tell me I was Luna's father?"

"I knew I was going to tell you and I didn't want to confuse the whole issue. I had to determine how you felt about me, before I brought a child into the whole dynamic."

"I've always loved you," Bjorn said. "And that won't change. But you have to understand, this has been a huge surprise for me and I'm just trying to understand everything."

"So just to make sure," Remus said, "You are not my mom, no more surprises."

Karen was shaking her head. Then Bjorn said, "Remus, your mom's name is Sarah, and I'm sorry, son, but she died while you and Romy were being born."

Who is Romy," Luna asked.

"That is my twin brother."

"Man, this is blowing my mind," Luna said as she put her hands up to the sides of her head. "So where is this . . . Romy?"

"He's still at home, he couldn't make this trip, but there is so much we need to talk about. But understand one thing, Luna, I am your father and if everything works out I want to be as important a part of your life as you will let me."

"Remus, I'm not trying to replace your mom," Karen said. "But if you would allow it, I would like to be your adopted mom."

The group tabled the rest of the talk, realizing that it would take a lot more conversations before they would have even a slight understanding of this bomb that had been dropped on them. Karen and Bjorn went for a walk down the beach, while Remus and Luna started to catch up.

"Are you doing okay?" he said.

"Yeah, I'm okay, but this crazy week has been a lot for me to get used to."

"I know."

"It's just that I've become okay with living and being alone, that it will take a lot of time to get back into living with someone."

"And you have to understand, that I, too, have I been dealing with single parenthood in a much more demanding environment."

"It will be especially difficult for our kids to adapt to this change," Karen said.

"I totally understand that, but Luna is my child. I'm not taking anything from the hard work you have done, but I am now ready to stand up and take my part in raising her."

"You are right, Luna is now your child as well as mine."

"There is another thing that I haven't discussed with you."

"And what is that?" she asked, waiting for the other shoe to drop.

"Just before this whole thing went down, Romy took me to a place where he had found something. It turned out to be a mammoth tusk."

"What, are you kidding me?"

"No, but that's not the end of the story."

Karen grinned because this story just kept getting better and better and she was sure that even when she thought she knew everything, she wouldn't.

"Yes?" Karen asked.

"When we dug the tusk out, a gold nugget about half the size of a golf ball came out."

"Holy shit, are you living on a gold mine?"

"It's impossible to say, but a nugget like that couldn't exist alone."

"Wow, so now I know why you have been torn between staying here and returning to the Northwest Territories."

"Well, you have to know that if I could cash in on this score, I could solve a lot of problems in my life."

"What problems?"

"I could get Romy some real professional help, I could send Remus to school for a real education, and I could take care of the scars that I've been living with for the last twenty years."

"So now I can appreciate the conundrum you have been dealing with."

"Yeah, so I'm torn, because I would love to just stay here with you, but there's all this money sitting up there, however, acquiring it would take me away from here and I would need heavy machinery to get to it."

"Well, wouldn't you dig up the land you love?"

"That's another thing. I don't officially own that land."

"Look, we stumbled unto each other and it felt like a dream come true, but I was afraid that you still had a need for wanderlust."

"Come on, Karen, I now have a daughter, and if that won't change someone, nothing will."

"But, look, I can't have you coming into Luna's life and then leaving to go chase an adventure. She really wants to keep you in her life."

"Karen, I have changed a lot since I was younger, I've matured more then I could show you."

"Well, you were definitely emotionally immature back then."

"I know, but aren't all men like that when they turn eighteen?"

"Yes, but I'm now responsible for a young mind, and I'm terrified that your leaving might be hard on her."

"Okay, if you can pay for a flight back to my home I will spend the summer trying to pan as much gold from the tundra as I can. I'm not talking about heavy machinery. I'll just use simple things. I will also try to come to a conclusion on what to do about Romy, and then when fall flies I will return here."

"What about Remus?"

"I think I'm going to have to take him back with me, because two of us could double our take."

"Have you thought of how you are going to get a bunch of gold across the border and onto a plane to fly back here?"

"No, I haven't figured out everything, but I will."

"What about Luna?" Karen asked.

Bjorn shook his head in silence, as they walked back to the area where the kids were. He felt an immense sense of pride when he saw his two kids chatting and laughing there in the sand.

"Hi, kids," Bjorn said.

"Dad, we're not kids," Remus replied.

Luna laughed at the statement that Remus had made.

"Okay, well, your mom and I have made a decision. Remus, you and I are going to return to the Northwest Territories," he said to a chorus of no's.

"Why? You just got here," Luna protested.

"Well, we aren't going to leave immediately, but probably within a week or two."

"But why, Dad?"

"We have some work to do, and then we will be able to return here forever."

"But I like it here, why can't we just stay here?"

"Your dad wants to bring your brother here," Karen said.

"Well, why can't I stay here while you go get Romy?"

"I might need your help."

"Romy can help you, this is the first time I've ever been on vacation, and Luna is going to teach me how to surf."

"Okay, well, let's talk about it and we will decide in about a week."

"Yeah, if Remus stays here it will guarantee that you will come back to be my dad," Luna said.

"I am your dad."

"And don't you forget it," Karen said.

"I couldn't possibly forget my daughter," Bjorn said smiling.

Luna smiled and felt a hole in her life had just been filled.

"Look, Luna, you've got me as long as you can handle me and I am head over heels in love with your mom and you."

The group headed back to the house and prepared a gourmet dinner. Everything here was strange to Remus, and Bjorn knew that he had been raised like a feral child, and Bjorn was worried about how modern society was going to affect him.

CHAPTER **43**

Luna went to her room and Remus crashed on the couch. Karen and Bjorn retired to her room. He was nervous because their relationship was riding on this night. Since he was leaving soon he had to make this the night that would reset an entire life. A life that should have been spent together. The pressure to succeed was intense, but Bjorn had spent a life with this kind of pressure. But it had been fifteen years since he had been with a woman. There were not a lot of available women up in the Territories.

He knew he had to be emotionally connected to this woman who he hadn't seen for twenty-two years. Then he started to lose his composure. The very tough guy fell apart, and for the first time in a long time the warrior sobbed as the tears flowed unabated for thirty minutes. That answered the question of emotions. But it did nothing for his sexual acumen—he was a babbling baby. The very intelligent scientist also started weeping, and she surrounded the man in her arms in a tight hug. That first night was just remembering the closeness from the past that was brief but stuck with him his entire life. The two had switched roles, with her taking the role as the supporter and he taking the role as the one being supported. The feeling of a naked female body next to him was intoxicating.

EPILOGUE

Karen took Bjorn to the airport, two weeks later. It had been a two-week vacation that she couldn't have imagined. He was an incredibly caring, giving man and a passionate lover that took her above and beyond any thing she had experienced.

He walked into the terminal and they had another very passionate kiss, which definitely got the attention of the other passengers. They didn't care who was seeing them or what they thought.

She watched as the plane took to the air and disappeared into the brightness of the Sun.

That's when Karen thought, *The Sun is what started all this and returned my lover to me and now it just took him away. As much as I love that flaming orb, it can be a cruel part of our lives.*

When Karen drove into the parking lot of the Mees Observatory the next evening, she jumped out of her car and gave Hoku a big hug.

"Thank you so much for helping us out while I was away," Karen said.

"You are welcome, Miss Karen."

"Well, I have to get to work," she said, as she walked into the observatory.

Then as she walked to the front doors, Hoku said, "Father Sun is talking."

She froze in her steps and then spun around and ran back to Hoku.

"What did you say?"

"My grandmother told me that Father Sun told her that a big happening is coming from the darkness," he said as he pointed to the dark sky.

"What kind of happening?" she asked.

"I do not know, but I've heard the nighttime scientists talking about it."

"Okay, thank you, Hoku," she said somewhat shocked, but she knew that Hoku and his people had special skills of observation. She walked into the observatory and bumped into one of the celestial astronomers from the night crew.

"Welcome back, Karen," he said.

"Thanks. Are you guys tracking any events right now?"

"Well, there's an asteroid we've been watching for about a year, but we don't think it's going to be anything to get excited about. But, hey, you had quite the time in D.C., but you couldn't do anything to prevent this disaster."

Karen just smiled and walked into her office and got on her computer, which showed her everything that was done since she was here last. That's when she saw it, an asteroid named Asolepius, she did a lot of research on this and caught up on the latest happenings. She decided to make a point to get more info from Hoku on her way out.

The major event was that the rolling blackout had taken out the power grid for half the nation, and power companies were installing new transformers.

At the end of the day she was walking out to the parking lot. There was a new security guard standing in the guard building and Karen walked over to him.

"Where's Hoku?"

"Oh, you mean the guy who used to work here? He quit, something about a family emergency."

Karen just turned and looked at the setting Sun with a blank look on her face.

"Karen?"

She spun around and was staring into the eyes that she had hoped she would never have to face again.

"Oh, hi, Warren," she said, "Or is it Jerry today?"

He smiled a short grin. "You can call me Warren."

"Since that's probably a fabrication, too?"

"Karen, you're such a whiny bitch."

"Oh, so no more mister nice guy, the gloves are off."

"Well, Karen, we are unsure if you had any involvement in Director McKenzie's death."

"Well, I've heard that the KGB agent was responsible for that."

"And where did you hear that?"

"The newspaper."

"And you had nothing to do with it?"

Karen tired of the conversation because he was obviously fishing for a confession. Then she noticed a movement out of the corner of her eye. A mountain of a man was silently approaching from behind Warren. Karen's heart jumped up into her throat. It was undeniably Hoku. Warren didn't see or hear anything.

The End

You gain strength, courage, and confidence by every experience in which you really stop to look fear in the face.

- Eleanor Roosevelt

AUTHOR'S NOTE

Everything in this novel is a reality and could happen. CMEs are solar storms that create fantastic aurora borealis displays. Even though they are beautiful, a major solar storm could also create a real threat to our way of life. Major solar storms can be seen as far south as Texas. If a power failure rolled across the United States, it could devastate people's lifestyle. A major power failure did occur in 1989 and started in Ontario. Satellites can fall out of orbit and space debris hits the Earth on an average of once every three weeks. Most space debris falls into oceans or uninhabitable regions of the land masses of the Earth. Some of the locations in this novel are fictitious because of the demands of the plot. And in 1989, the Hudson Bay setting of this novel was in the Northwest Territories. Since then the additional Canadian province of Nunavut has been established and now includes the setting.